THE
WORLD
ON FIRE

THE WORLD BURNS - BOOK 8

BOYD CRAVEN

TABLE OF CONTENTS

CHAPTER 1

King, Michael, Chad, Rose and Anna Lewiston stopped their APC for the third time of the day. Diesel fuel was difficult to find and siphon, so they'd started finding all the small fuel cans they could and got it two to five gallons at a time and transferred it between stalled semi-trucks and the APC.

"Do you think we'll get there today?" Rose asked Chad, her hand snaking through his.

"Should, as long as the last twenty miles are not like they were going through that last city," he said in broken English.

Michael smiled and called over his shoulder, "Can one of you radio them? I don't know how close I'm getting and I don't want drive right up and have them think we're out to hurt them."

BOYD CRAVEN

He'd gotten good at driving the APC, taking every chance he could to learn from Chad, getting to know everything about it. They'd left for the trip to Kentucky to 'The Homestead', but had stopped several times, the last time for three weeks.

It wasn't that they were far off, it was more that they had found people who had been in desperate need of help. Twice, Michael, King and Chad had used the APC to bust through roadblocks or run through houses where raiders, for a lack of a better term, had holed up and held the citizens hostage. Sometimes literally. Whenever they found problems like those, they couldn't turn a blind eye. They had all been in the camps, and seen how bad it was.

One of the surprising things they'd heard was that the FEMA camps they had been in in Alabama were some of the worst run. Lukashenko wasn't just a sadistic bastard; he was also corrupt. If word of his and his men's misdeeds hadn't been handled by NATO, they would have hanged him. The biggest mind blower was the President coming on the radio and making his announcement. It was laced with some of the most outlandish opinions, information and good intel. If everyone was supposed to report in... King and Chad were already considered criminals for one reason or another... But King had wanted to go to Kentucky to help out.

There was something restless about him lately and he wouldn't talk to Michael about it.

"I'll do it," Anna, Michael's mother said and picked up the mic.

4

THE WORLD ON FIRE

"Homestead, this is Anna Lewiston. Do you copy? Over."

"Anna Lewiston, this is base security. We read you, over."

"Base security for Homestead Kentucky? Where Mr. Blake is? Over?"

"Affirmative. What can we do for you Miss Lewiston? Over."

"We're heading that direction with a captured APC. It does not have guns nor turrets. Our intentions are peaceful and we'd like to join the crowd. Over."

"Give me your markings."

She looked at King who wrote them down and she read them off.

"Affirmative. We've been tracking your progress for twenty minutes. Please stop next to that blue trailer, over."

Michael was already acting on the instructions, but his eyes had gone wide. If they had been following their progress for this entire time…

"We're parked," she said and hung up the microphone.

"Pop your hatch, over."

King did and sat down. His bulk covered most of one bench seat and he made sure to put his hands on his legs, palms down. Michael was going to get his pistols out and put them down, but there was already movement outside and a face looked in at him through the viewing port, startling him. It was a young woman, clean, her hair tucked into a cam-

5

ouflage hat. A noise at the hatch had him spinning to see a form drop in, an M4 at the ready.

"Hands in front," she said in a friendly voice, but her eyes were everywhere, looking at everyone.

They all complied, and Rose was having a hard time holding still. That had been a mild annoyance to King; the young woman was full of energy, and being cooped up in a hot metal box all day had done little good for her nerves. Now having an armed woman covering her had her almost wetting herself. It was fast and unexpected.

"Anybody armed?" She asked as two more figures dropped in through the hatch.

One of them immediately pressed the button to open the back door, and it started moving out slowly, the heavy armor preventing the hydraulics from going any faster.

Everybody said yes except Rose, and they held their hands up, to show they weren't going for weapons.

"Good, it's a rough world out there," she said, putting her MR over her shoulder on the sling, "My name's Corrine, I'm a member of the Squad, part of the Homestead's scouting teams. You guys can relax. Let's just step out into the light and talk a minute."

The other women didn't say anything, and they'd held their M4s down low, but at the ready.

"Slick," King said, ducking as he exited.

"Better than I expected," Michael said, following the big man out and then stuttered to a stop as

6

THE WORLD ON FIRE

he realized they were surrounded by twenty heavily armed men and woman, some of whom had RPG launchers trained on them.

"We've had our share of problems," Corrinne said and then nodded to them.

"Let's put your guns down and then I can call everyone off here and we can talk. It makes everyone less nervous."

"If we don't want to?" King asked.

"We'll ask you to turn around and head away from the Homestead."

"Fair," King replied, and slowly disarmed.

He hadn't worn shirts much since the break out and rescue of the other FEMA camp. Instead, he wore a tactical vest loaded with all sorts of lethal goodies. He also carried a duffel, but he'd left that in the APC. He stripped out of his vest instead of going piece by piece, and then dropped his web belt with his pistols. Lastly, he pulled a stiletto out of his boot and put it in the pile. Seeing the big man disarm, the others followed suit. Michael slowly pulled out his father's Gold Cups and lowered them to the ground.

"A two-gun type of kid, huh?" Corrine asked.

Michael just shrugged.

"Cat got your tongue?" another woman asked.

"No ma'am, just nervous," he admitted.

"Why you nervous, sugar?" a redhead asked him, "You got something to be nervous about?"

"If what I heard on the radio is right, we've got twenty guns on us. I heard about the squad. You

BOYD CRAVEN

guys are supposed to be the..." he swallowed, "top dogs. Trained by Blake's wife. So yeah, twenty guns in my face by hardened killers tends to make me want to piss myself." The words came out in a rush and Michael, horrified, immediately wanted to take them back, but his mother burst out laughing.

"That is pretty funny," Corrine said and made a motion for everyone to lower their guns.

"Truth is, we never know now a days who's who. We were tasked with following your APC because it's got the markings of some of Eastern Europeans who were running camps down south. Didn't know if you were friendlies or not."

"Fair enough. I'm Corrine, this is Melissa. Sgt. Smith?"

"Yes Ma'am." A young but competent-looking man stepped forward.

"What do you think?" she asked.

"I think we found the folks from Alabama and Louisiana," he said with a grin. "Smith," he said, holding out his hand to King.

"King," he replied and shook, and soon everyone was greeting each other.

It didn't bother anyone that the guns were within reach; they were outnumbered. When introductions were done they rearmed themselves and several people, including Corinne, got into the APC for the last part of the trip to the homestead.

"The roads, how did you...?" Michael said after they had been on the road for almost twenty minutes.

8

THE WORLD ON FIRE

Like magic, the roadway had been cleared, with dead cars lined up neatly on the furthest edge of the shoulder, leaving the lanes open.

"We've been working on clearing the roads in our area for a month now," Sgt. Smith said.

"Smart," King told him.

"He don't talk much, does it?" Corrinne asked Rose.

"No, not really," she said.

"Nyet," Chad said, "unless it's to show us something."

"Talk too much, mouth gets you into trouble," King explained.

"That's the most I've heard him say in a while," Anna said with a smile.

Corrine and Smith talked into their radios quietly and they were stopped at the end of Holloway Lane by an armored APC with a 30mm cannon pointed at them.

"End of the trip for now. Leave the keys in the ignition and we'll hoof the rest of it," Corrinne said, squeezing to the back and hitting the button to open the rear door.

"It doesn't—"

"Don't," King said softly, his voice deep but calm, "They'll have it for us when we leave."

"Yes, we just can't fit it up the roadway," Corinne said, "Trust me, it'll be secure here."

§ § §

BOYD CRAVEN

They were walking up the gentle slope of the two track, marveling at the canopy of trees. Michael and his mom talked about what they wanted out of this, and they were almost in agreement. Michael had wanted to head south and towards the fight when he was done, but Anna hadn't. She thought she'd be more helpful doing what she could from behind the lines, at least a good couple of states away, and she had begged Michael to do the same.

"I can't do that, Mom," he complained, "It's just… I've changed. I can't let something like this happen, not if I can help it."

"Save the world yourself?" King asked.

"No, but I have to… I don't know. I have to act, move, help. If I don't, it's going to drive me crazy."

"I wish you wouldn't, but you've pulled off some crazy stuff before. Lord knows I would have stopped you if I had known it, but I'm glad to have you back," she said, pulling him close in a hug.

King stopped walking, and in turn everyone else stopped to see what had caught his eye. He walked over to the side of the trees and put a large finger into several of the holes that pock marked them. He looked down and then across the way to the other trees.

"Traps," he said.

"No, there used to be, but they're all disarmed now. Blake did that back when the EMP first hit. Lots of people wanting to move to the country, eat a lot of peaches…"

"Michael and Anna cracked up but King and

10

THE WORLD ON FIRE

Rose looked at her, puzzled.

"Going to move out in the country, going to eat a lot of peaches," Chad sang in an off-key, broken English accent, "What? It's the Presidents of the United States of America. Is good song, you like?"

Everyone stood in awkward silence for a moment and then busted up. King moved onto the next tree that had been peeled by buckshot and started walking again, trusting Corrinne, who was walking at the front of the group.

§ § §

Sandra and Blake had been waiting for the new arrivals. They had managed the growth of the Homestead, and set up incubator operations in four parts of the state. With Blake being the Director of FEMA for Kentucky, he'd used his position to educate and show by example. It was a good program and it was working well. By wintertime, many families would be saved instead of maybe freezing to death or being picked off by lone wolf raiders.

"John told me about these guys a while back," Sandra said putting her arms around her husband's side and hugging him close.

"Yeah, I remember hearing it on the radio. The break out. That was them?" he asked.

"Some of them. I'd like to meet them."

"He kicked again," Blake said, feeling the baby moving in his wife's swollen stomach.

"He has been for a while now," she murmured,

BOYD CRAVEN

"I just don't... Oh, my God!" She broke off.

Walking up the hill was The Squad with the travelers. They were well fed and armed for bear, but it was the giant-sized black man that got her attention.

"KING?" She yelled and started running as fast as her body allowed her.

CHAPTER 2

NEAR BRACKETTVILLE, TEXAS –
BRAD PALMER

L adies and Gentlemen," the voice began, and everyone sat up straight as the 44th President of the United States, the one believed to be dead, spoke. "*I come here tonight, as your President and as a fellow human being, to talk to the citizens of our great nation.*

I'd like, first and foremost," he paused for a moment, "*to talk about the attack. There have been several points of misinformation circulating. We were not attacked by Iran, Saudi Arabia, Iraq, Afghanistan or Syria, despite what others have reported. They do not have the information that I do. It is true that the nuclear talks were going badly, but it wasn't a single country that did this to us.*

Elements of ISIS and North Korea detonated a nuclear weapon over the United States of America in the guise of a satellite launch, using a mobile sea platform. The resulting EMP has destroyed key critical infrastructure throughout most of the Continental United States, sparing some regions in the Pacific Northwest and Alaska. Our Canadian friends have suffered as well, in regions of Ontario and Quebec.

The regions of Mexico that have been touched by the EMP have already been experiencing destabilization from cartel violence, but they have not experienced the losses that we Americans have. It's brutal, it's horrible and the reason you are not seeing the United States Military take more action within the country is because we are now fighting a war on two fronts.

First, the war against North Korea has begun once again, as the Korean Armistice Agreement has been nullified. They've launched attacks against Washington DC, Maryland, and other parts of the Eastern seaboard. Even now, their subs try to sneak through our defensive networks. As we recall our military from around to globe to help in the naval battles, our country is being attacked from within.

There were elements in several cities, Dearborn and Ann Arbor Michigan for example, where there were radical religious factions that acted with the knowledge of the coming attack, and destabilized the region. Those citizens and immigrants are being dealt with by a large force that has come down from Camp Grayling and from all over the Midwest. Acts of violence, terrorism and hate crimes are running rampant throughout the country. The racial violence

14

THE WORLD ON FIRE

in the States is staggering and, if there was ever a time for Americans to pull together, now is that time. Remember, neither race nor religion is a good enough reason to take up arms against your fellow humans.

There are, of course, more militant factions within the country; those who are born with radical conservative views who have openly refused orders and even attacked government agents and their leadership.

"*These factions will be stamped out and their leadership brought to justice. We will not tolerate former members of our armed services openly mocking and attacking the government in their own homes and cities,*" he paused for a moment before continuing.

"*As some of you may have already realized or heard, each Governor of the State has had the National Guard activated. All current and former service members between the ages of 18 and 65 are required to report for duty or evaluation at the nearest National Guard outpost. I have heard reports of units going rogue and how things were settled, as the intelligence comes in to me slowly... but it will not be tolerated. Military members will report for duty, or be prosecuted per executive order. Those men and women who betrayed their oaths... You will be dealt with as well.*

Law Enforcement – I know many of you, like so many of the National Guard Units, have had to go home now to protect your families. It was your duty as a husband, wife, parent or guardian. Now it is time to guard our country, our cities, and our way of life. You are to report back to your stations and precincts where you will be resupplied by the FEMA emergency managers, who report to the Governors and myself. Martial Law is in effect until lifted by Executive Order, and all elections have been suspended.

"I..." the President paused again, "I really hope to suspend Martial Law as quickly as I can, because my advisors now tell me that over 80% of the country has died off in four separate waves. Those very sick or on life support, the ones taking life-saving medications, further more from disease and starvation and lastly from human predation. I am asking everyone to assist with the rebuilding efforts, and for your cooperation with the Governors of the State.

For those of you still in FEMA camps, I urge you to stay and continue the work. Some have told me that they've been called the equivalent of labor camps, or even concentration camps. I do not agree with that assessment. The horrors of a few isolated instances does not paint the picture of the entire effort of FEMA and NATO to help our nation getting kick started again. Without the labor to build critical components, we cannot pull ourselves out of the ashes. Instead of going to work, we're asking the people we're taking care of in the camps to do their part in contributing to rebuild our country.

Again, attacks against those camps will not be tolerated, and those who instigate or support them will be brought to justice." The words chilled everyone in the room. "I want to stress to you; those in

16

THE WORLD ON FIRE

the camps are not prisoners, they are there to help with rebuilding key infrastructure, designed to help the population out."

"...That is why with great regret, I have one last sad piece of news. The South West of the country is being invaded, for lack of a better term, by a private army whose members are from all over the world, seemingly financed by agents of ISIS and North Korea, being guided into the country by the Cartels. Texas, New Mexico, Arizona and parts of California are now open battlefields. There is very little information to go on right now and, even if I had it, I could not share it openly before verifying its sources. We believe it to be the start..." The President made another long pause, *"We believe it's the start of a land campaign the likes of which Americans haven't seen in many lifetimes. As soon as our Navy and Airforce bring personal and equipment back, they will be pressed into service defending our borders and key infrastructure.*

My fellow Americans, it is now time to take back our country and pull ourselves out of the ashes of a charred existence. I will be in touch. God Bless."

The church went silent for several moments and then everyone began speaking at once. The noise was insane, and I couldn't make out any individual voices. The pastor had promised the congregation a radio broadcast by the president, and oh boy, did he deliver!

There were quite a few people who had working radios and transportation. I was one of those lucky

17

enough to have a form of transportation, but only if you like to eat bugs. My truck was dead in the water the day the EMP happened. I'd been hooking up the trailer to it for a Saturday hunt. I was supposed to have been a paid guide for some folks from up north to hunt feral hogs and javelin. It wasn't a big deal; I'd planned to take them out to a farm near the deer lease and let them take some long distance pot shots and help them pack up their kill before they turned and went back up to Indiana or wherever it was they said they came from. Five hundred dollars for half a day's work, and the farmer paid me a bounty of fifty dollars for every dead hog.

I know that was double dipping it a bit, but I'd always considered myself a young entrepreneur who had an expensive habit. I loved my truck, I loved my dirt bike and quads, and I loved my guns. I was more than a little shocked when I heard more than saw everything get fried. There wasn't much electronic in my buddy Stu's house, but when the radio fell silent, the lights went out and everything smelled like ozone on a hot summer's eve, I knew something was up.

"Let's go man, this is going to get ugly," Stuart said, bumping my shoulder with his.

"All right man," I told him, "We still going to Randolph's house?" I asked.

"Yeah, drive us by there," Stuart said, "Before we head home."

We made our exit slowly. I didn't have to hear individual voices to know what everyone was talk-

THE WORLD ON FIRE

ing about. The invasion. We'd felt rather safe, being so close to the air force base, but little things were starting to happen. Theft had gone through the roof. In town last week alone, somebody had stolen a ham I'd had hanging in a makeshift smoker that Stuart put together. Stealing food was pretty much a capital crime at this point, and the world had gotten so scary that people coming onto your property without permission were often times met over the sights of a gun if you didn't know them.

Not that town was large. I actually lived outside of town, and had three neighbors. That was a pretty sweet deal when the world was normal and sane, but it sucked horribly now. Going anywhere took gas, and that had become one of the key barter items. Gas, ammunition and food. Food itself was getting hard to find. I'd been lucky that Stuart was home on leave when the EMP hit, because I'd had a group of people try to come and take by force just about everything I held dear.

It hadn't been a week after the grid went down that I heard something in the garage. Being the dumbass I was, I headed out through the laundry room in my boxers, without a gun. There was a light in the garage and that had puzzled my sleep-addled brain, until I'd realized that the garage door had been jimmied open and there were five men working on pushing the three quads and two dirt bikes I used on my paid hunts down the driveway. I'd called out to them, and three of them had scattered. Two had pulled guns, and suddenly the only thing between me and them was a hair's breadth of space.

A form came out of the darkness behind them and the slide racking of a pump action twelve gauge made them look back to find Stu ready and willing to start the dance. That incident had happened almost three or four months ago – time has been funny since every day is the same now – but walking out of the church, I'm reminded of it because I've got three assholes surrounding my quad, and one of them has the cover open, exposing the wires.

"Really? Gonna hotwire a fourwheeler?" I asked, drawing my 1911, my backup gun when I go hunting.

"This is ours," a thick Spanish accent replied, definitely not a local. The accent didn't even sound Mexican, more south American.

"No, that's mine," I said, pissed that the gun pointing at them wasn't scaring them off.

I'd been spared having to shoot anybody ever, but Stuart blurred into motion. He was dressed like he always did, boots, jeans and plaid shirt. The rangy look was deceptive, trust me, I know from experience… because he was also fast, and he knew how to fight dirty. His fist swung out, clipping the man sitting on the seat and making him pitch off into the two that were on the other side. Since we'd been the first out of the church, I also figured we were the only people about. Great. No backup and Stu had picked a fight with three when there were only two of us.

THE WORLD ON FIRE

"You're dead," the man spat, reaching into his waistband.

Gun? Hello, I already had one out... Maybe they didn't see me as a threat? I squeezed the trigger. In the darkness the flames that shot out of the .45 were bright and would have blinded me if it was full dark and not just getting there. The bullet ricocheted off the pavement and off into the scrub in the distance and everyone froze for a moment, considering me.

I'm not much, young, thinner than my normal because lack of food and dietary choices and, at twenty four, I'm often told I don't even look eighteen sometimes. That used to be funny, but now it was working against me as one of the dudes gave a laugh and reached for his waist again. A revolver cocking made everyone pause, including me. Stuart had pulled his .44 and was holding the big gun on the three Hispanic men.

"My friend here gave you a warning shot. I won't. Light up out of here before I bury you in a shallow ditch somewhere," Stuart spat.

"What's going on?" Somebody shouted from behind us, and I recognized the voice.

"This isn't over," the man Stu punched said through bloodstained lips.

"Yes it is, because if I see any of you again, I'll put a bullet into you," Stuart told them, ignoring Pastor Steve's voice from behind us.

I could hear the murmur of voices, but I never moved and kept my gun trained on them. I knew at least one of them had a gun; one for sure had a

21

wicked looking hunting knife strapped to his belt.

"What is going on?" Pastor Steve shouted, repeating himself.

"They're trying to steal our ride," I said.

"Not on church property! Do not…" his words cut off, and he must have moved somewhere behind me but I never turned to look.

"What's it going to be, guys?" I asked them, knowing I couldn't pull the trigger, but I kept my father's old gun trained on them anyways.

One of them spat on the ground, and as one, they turned and started walking. It was silent for long several moments and I could hear the voices of the small town's congregation behind us talking. When the three men were out of range, I holstered the .45 and turned to face the pastor.

"You brought guns to a house of God? I know you both, and I've asked you please not to bring firearms into the service. They're dangerous!"

"This wasn't a service, preacher," Stuart said, "And guns aren't dangerous, they're tools. One you should probably learn how to use with your church in the middle of nowhere."

"I'd never… you can't… I won't have it. I do not want firearms on the church property. Those things are dangerous, despite what you boys have said over and over… Do you all hear me?" His words thundered in volume at the end.

A couple of good men came and stood at our side, pushing their shirts away from their waists, exposing their pistols as well.

THE WORLD ON FIRE

"Looks like we won't be welcome either then?" the eldest Garcia brother asked. George? Jorge? I couldn't remember what he went by, I only knew him from the services when my parents were still alive and had dragged me along when we had a Texan as a preacher, not some lily-livered Democrat from Chicago. He was five or six years older than his brother, if I remembered correctly.

"You? You both?" The pastor sputtered.

"Lots more than him, Pastor Steve," I said, "and I bet you every pickup truck still running has at least one rifle in the rack." I turned so I could see his expression.

His liberal views might have gone over in a big city like Dallas or San Antonio, but down here near the border of Mexico, we'd all been taking bets on how far he'd make it before he asked for a re-assignment. Pastor Bill and his wife Miss Sally had been here until two years ago when he up and retired.

"Yeah, there's a few of us, Pastor. If you have an outright ban, I don't think there'll be much in the way of people to come to your service. World's gotten to be a dangerous place," Ramone Garcia said.

Him I remembered for sure; we'd played football together in Brackettville. He was often the linebacker for the team, whereas I was one of many receivers. He was built like Stuart, tall and strong. He could speak English fluently, without an accent. He wasn't an immigrant, his family lived here when Texas joined the union. There's a lot of folk like that, and there's a lot of bigotry in the worked but

23

BOYD CRAVEN

it wasn't something we put up with here. Most of us had Spanish blood of some sort, unless we were imports like Pastor Steve.

The Pastor sputtered and I shook my head and sat on the quad. No wires had been cut, but I could see they were looking to bypass the kill switch in the ignition and then all it would taken was them touching the ignition wire to a hot wire and it would have been running. But the steering still would have been locked, and I have no idea how they would have gotten around that... The stupidity of my fellow human beings shocked me sometimes. I knew it shouldn't, but Darwin's law never seemed to apply to stupidity.

"Did they mess it up?" Stuart asked, putting the hand cannon he was holding back into the holster.

"Naw," I said, locking the cover back into place and putting the key in.

It was my older quad, almost no electronics on it, and no lights that worked. Just a brush guard and a pull start.

"Let's get out of here. If the pastor is too stupid to realize the world..."

I let Stu drone on as he swung into the seat behind me. I could still hear him, but he was ranting about gun control, the stupidity of people who advocated it for the wrong reasons, the mental health laws... I took off, the knobby tires making a quiet rumble on the pavement. We had to go visit the mayor and, if we wanted to be home before it got extremely late, we'd need to hurry. We'd built him

24

THE WORLD ON FIRE

a fancy goat pen at the edge of the small city in exchange for some gas and dried foods that the city had in stores from the last FEMA group that had come through.

No camps for us Texans. I remembered hearing about the FEMA camps and the President's words on the radio address. I hadn't even heard of camps... Just the FEMA representative saying help was coming soon... Other than the truck full of dried food, the man hadn't been able to tell us much or help us much. It sounded like the government was coming out of hiding. Finally. If it weren't for the occasional truck from Laughlin AFB, I'd almost think we'd have something to be worried about.

According to the President, we did. Maybe we were just too far off the beaten path, but other than some minor violence and thefts from drifters, it had been a sleepy summer. I'd been doing more to scrounge up food than keep in touch with world events though. In no time at all, I turned onto the road that led up to the small ranch the mayor owned. He had just a couple of bulls and a few cows, having sold his stock up in the spring time.

"Lights are still on," I said, turning the quad off and climbing off.

"Yeah," Stuart said, quiet and probably pissed that I'd tuned him out.

We'd been friends since my Junior year of high school and, when my parents died, I moved in with him so I could finish up and think about college. Instead, I went a little wild. I worked when I felt like it, hunted every moment I could and, when I found out I could make money hunting, it was a match made in heaven. Stuart had bought a house, was settling down to marry a beautiful woman… Life was easy, until things fell apart for him. Maria left him after an argument I never heard about, and he ended up enlisting.

I kept the house up for him and he paid the taxes and part of the bills, I paid the other part… Only luck had him on leave from the Army when the EMP hit, or God knows where he'd have been stranded. Probably someplace with power and air conditioning. He said even the tents in Afghanistan had air conditioning. How can a tent in a third world country have air conditioning when a house in the USA couldn't?

I let Stuart knock and stood back behind him. He was friends with the Mayor, and he'd gotten us the gig. I just hoped there was more work coming. The food helped a lot, but it wasn't going to be enough for the winter time. Both of us were a little food obsessed and missing being able to just go buy a Big Mac, an extra large Slurpee or even a Coke. God, I missed Coke.

"Hey boys," Randolph Stephens said, opening his door wide to let us in, "I'm glad you came. Did you hear the President's address?"

"Yes sir," We both chorused.

"Good, good. I'd like to ask you two about a job I have in mind. Might have you gone for a week or more, but you'd have food provided for you while

THE WORLD ON FIRE

you're gone, and something for the leaner months." He glanced down at my jeans that had been cinched tight, the new holes in my belt evident.

"Sure," we both said, following him to the kitchen table.

"Sit, let's hash this out. Anybody care for a Coke?"

I smiled; maybe there was a God after all.

CHAPTER 3

King's head snapped up at hearing the shout, to see a woman he had thought dead running towards him. Her stomach was swollen with baby and a look of surprise was etched on her features. As she neared him, she launched herself and the big man caught her with one arm as she threw her arms around his neck and hugged the life out of him.

"How can this be?" he asked, putting her down and pushing her hair out of her eyes.

The woman he remembered had always had a short if not buzzed cut, and she had gone from whipcord thin to pregnant and curvy with hair down to her chin. Despite the differences though, he recognized his apprentice at once.

"I thought you were dead!" he whispered to her,

THE WORLD ON FIRE

"They told me you went down in Afghanistan on the next mission and you were killed by the insurgents."

"I'm glad to see you," she said burying her face into his chest and trying to squeeze him to death.

She broke off and turned to find Blake standing about ten feet back, a puzzled expression on his face.

"Blake, this is King; he was my mentor and teacher."

Blake walked forward slowly, his hand extended. His wife had opened up a little to him, but it was when she was sleeping that she let things slip. Missions that didn't involve helicopters or mechanics. He'd heard as much from Boss Hogg's men who tried to abduct her, but here it was in the flesh, almost 300 or 350 pounds of it.

"Thank you," Blake said, his hand dwarfed by the giant's.

"Did my job," King told him.

Blake was tall, but King was a giant, and although they weren't eye to eye, it was a close thing. Blake didn't feel any menace coming from him and relaxed even further.

"If you hadn't done it so well, I might not have ever met her," he told him.

"She's my best student. Got better than me a long time ago."

Duncan picked that time to walk up and take in the scene as the rest of the group gathered around and stared in shock.

29

BOYD CRAVEN

"Let's make introductions. My name is Chad, this is my fiancée Rose, my comrade Michael Lewiston and his mom Anna," Chad said, as clearly as he could.

"I'm Blake," he said shaking hands. "I'm not here for long, but I think we've got some talking to do. Anybody hungry?"

They nodded.

§ § §

They never told Blake everything, but a lot of the general holes in Sandra's time had been filled in. There were operations where the quick insertion of a person who could get out of sticky situations was needed. The military had been training people for special missions for a long time, but when they needed to find a woman to fit a specific mission profile, Sandra had been selected and sent to King for specialized training.

They heard how the quiet Kentucky woman ignored the idiocy that some of the men in uniform seemed to thrive on and instead focused on the training. Soon, the naysayers were trying to keep up. After a while, they struggled to even compete at anything near her level of competence and physical fitness. When it came to books she was quick, and she matched that with an uncanny ability to read people. She was admired and when she left training, people knew she would go on to make the country proud.

THE WORLD ON FIRE

John had been sent on one such mission and gotten stuck behind enemy lines. Sandra and her friend had stolen a chopper, rescued John and had almost had the Armed Forces Oversight Committee tied in knots in congressional hearings. To make things disappear, Sandra had died in a subsequent mission, ending the investigation. That hadn't really happened, but it worked long enough for her to leave the military and resume civilian life with a modified DD-214 and some papers that probably came from the CIA.

"How is it John didn't know you?" Blake asked quietly, "You were there with him."

"I was sheep dipped a long time ago. I knew him, he didn't know me." King said in a quiet rumble.

"What's that?" Anna asked.

"Erased from the records. I got to pick a new name and new record." King told her.

"King…" Michael said softly.

King nodded, "Sounds a lot better than what I was born with kid."

"And what are you looking to do here?" Blake asked King.

"Help," he said, putting a large piece of ham into his mouth and chewing.

"He can help us train," Sandra said quietly, "We've got a ton of new recruits coming in this week."

King shook his head and swallowed, "I will train if there's no one better, but I'd rather be in the field, doing what I do."

"He's talking a lot of words again," Rose whispered, and Anna shushed her.

"He goes in spurts," Sandra said smiling, "He's not one for wasting time or energy. Now, how did you two meet up?" she asked Michael, already knowing they were from the same camp.

"At the FEMA camp at the TCI," Michael said. "He was there when the EMP hit, I was only there maybe... a week?" Michael asked, looking to King for confirmation.

"You were locked up?" Sandra asked surprised, before King could respond, "For what?"

"Misunderstanding with cops," he said and shrugged.

"That sucks," Rose piped up and they all nodded.

§ § §

King and Michael worked out with the squad for the first week. King made some training suggestions to Duncan on the side and they were implemented. They hadn't wanted to stay a week, but Michael was insisting on going along with King. The young man had impressed him with his courage and natural ability so he agreed... but he wanted a chance for Michael to get some training time in, even if it was at the Homestead.

"Is there any chance I can talk you out of going all lone wolf?" Blake asked the two of them.

THE WORLD ON FIRE

"No," King replied.

Michael shook his head. "I just want to help. King and I threw in together a while back. We've been doing ok for a couple months now. It won't be horrible, and we'll have supply drops."

"Who filled you in, kid?" Blake said smiling.

"He's almost my age," Bobby said, walking up with Melissa on his arm.

"Sorry," Blake said, "Everyone just looks so young now... So there's no talking you two out of it?"

"No sir," King said quietly, "But I'd appreciate it if you can find Anna a good spot where she can help out and feel useful."

"I was going to see if she'd train here with David and Patty. We need more comms operators, and she sounds like she'd be a natural. Then send her to say... somewhere near Saint Louis at a temporary base? I dunno, that's more Sandra's thing, coordinating with the government."

"If you two can do that, I'd appreciate it," Michael told him.

"You almost finish each other's sentences," Blake grinned.

King and Michael both held their hands up and made the iffy gesture and laughed at Blake's expression.

"Fight together and kill together long enough, no words needed." King explained.

"Listen, I'm out of here. I'm not sure if I'll ever see you two again. I'd like to wish you good luck, and pray for your safe return," he said offering his hand to each of them.

"Thanks," Michael said for both of them.

Blake walked away, feeling conflicted about the young man heading off. Their plan was simple and would be devastating. It was something Sandra had been trying to get implemented for a long time. Small cells operating as sappers and saboteurs behind the enemy lines. Terrorizing the terrorists and the North Korean advisors that they'd heard so little about.

They would be out in the middle of nowhere, setting tricks and traps... being the furthest forward set of eyes anywhere. It was not something Blake would want for anybody, but this wasn't going to be a conventional fight, or a conventional war.

"Ready to practice some more?" King asked.

"No," Michael admitted, "but I need to. This is going to be... interesting."

"Chinese saying, "may you live in interesting times", he said quietly.

"Is that like a good luck, or a well wish?" Michael asked.

King chuckled, his deep voice booming, "No son," he said, "It's not."

"Huh, oh well."

Together they practiced grapples and throws. For a guy the size of Michael to control somebody who was both physically stronger and bigger, King was working on teaching him some combinations of Judo and Kendo, using the other person's mass

THE WORLD ON FIRE

and momentum against them. It had been a rough couple of days, ones that had left Michael sore. They had drawn a crowd today, as most of the recruits were worn out already. Most of it wasn't their fault; lack of nutrition and nowhere to openly train had left many a body out of shape.

Michael and King had already been in fighting shape, and now Michael was trying to learn enough hand to hand to not be a liability to King.

"Want to shoot?" King asked.

"I wouldn't mind learning some different guns," Michael admitted, "But for what we're doing, I think these are going to be enough." He patted the Colts.

He'd held onto his Grandfather's carbine, but had left it in the APC. He'd use that for heavier work, and instead he'd been gifted with an M4 from the growing Armory that Duncan and Bobby were working on.

"Good, need to do it and get out of here soon," King rumbled.

"Why, you got an itch to fight?" Michael grinned.

"In case you missed it, something's in the water," King grinned, something that didn't happen often and was now the second time in the conversation he'd shown amusement.

"What do you mean?" Michael asked.

"Everyone is hooking up here. So many single ladies. Three weddings planned this week. All the wives are heavy with child. If we don't leave now, we'll meet somebody, fall in love, get married, and plant petunias instead of fighting."

"Dude…." Michael said shaking his head and laughing at that mental picture, "No way. Besides, you're too old, I mean… I …"

"Kid," King said pointing a beefy finger at him, "I thought you were done with PT."

Michael got a serious look on his face and then busted up laughing. In fact, there had been many invitations to dinner, and he understood what the big man was talking about.

"I am. I get it, and I was kidding, it just came out wrong."

"Let's go eat," he said, closing the subject. "I'm hungry."

CHAPTER 4

SPAFFORD TEXAS – JOE

The radio crackled at his hip. "Hey Joe, you coming into Brackettville anytime soon?"

Joe stood and stretched, his joints popping. He was in fact Jose Greene, but Joe to his friends. He'd been born to a Hispanic mother and a father who was half Indian and half gringo. It had given him a unique perspective during his long life, one that was made interesting in his youth because of his mixture of heritage. Now, almost sixty seven, most people didn't care about things like they did decades ago when the marches for Civil Rights had swept the nation.

In the house he was born in, nobody cared much for who was what color, but suddenly it mattered, and when he'd been bussed into Brackettville for school, it mattered. Not so much the black versus white, but white versus Hispanic. Mostly though, it was a minor thing compared to other parts of the country. Only college took him away for a few years. He was going to be an accountant, somebody who could handle money and numbers. A noble profession he thought. His parents were devastated, wanting him to continue on with the farm they had built from literally nothing.

"I might, I have some animals to bring for trade." Joe said, smiling.

"Good, do you have enough for me to send a truck over?"

"You have gas?" Joe asked, surprised.

He had gas, and a working vehicle, but he kept it hidden and stashed in the small barn he had. If his friend had some to burn on this trip, he may have some sort of deal in mind. Since an EMP took out the power grid, things had gotten primitive and reports on the old HAM radios were conflicting at best, outright misinformation at worst.

"Yeah, I do. Do you think I could, uh… barter or trade for six or seven momma goats?"

"Those are my milkers," Joe told him.

"Can't be all of them. I'm trying to start something out this way. Oh yeah, over."

Joe smiled. Randy always forgot that, but other than the movement of people from Mexico north, it was quiet here. Hell, it'd been quiet in Spafford almost his entire life. There were less than 30 people alive in the town now and even before the EMP, there had only been about 80 people. The elderly

THE WORLD ON FIRE

and those dependent on medications were the first ones to die off, and these days hunger was setting in. The remaining people now relied on him and his goats for at least some nourishment beyond what they could grow or hunt.

"What are you thinking for trade?"

"You want to do this over the air?" Randolph asked.

"I don't want to burn gas I don't have, nor should you. Give me an idea here."

"Well, I could send a couple guys out there to work with you for a bit. You'd have to feed them, and I'd send provisions and the other trade goods you and I discussed in person the last time we were face to face."

Joe's feet clicked together as he repositioned himself and looked at the radio like it was a magical instrument. In a way it was; it was one of the only things working in town besides his solar water pumps and his 1976 police cruiser. He had a little harbor freight backpack solar setup he'd gotten for one of his grandkids' birthday. The EMP had prevented him from traveling or mailing it out, so he'd kept it for now to charge the batteries on his old police issue radio.

See, accounting was fun, but he needed more classes and the Sheriff's department had been hiring on deputies in Brackettville at a time he needed money… and it'd become a career, not a stopgap. He was now a retired Sheriff, but folks called him Chief all the time. Buying the old equipment for himself when the department upgraded had seemed like a frugal investment. One that had suddenly paid off big time.

"You were able to get the items I asked about?" Joe asked.

"Yes?" Randolph said, seemingly confused.

"And the ammunition for it?"

"Dammit Joe…"

"I dunno, six of my milkers—"

"You can't possibly drink that much milk! Besides, we want to breed them and start our own herd of them out here."

"Why not just go lasso you some of them beefalo things that are probably going wild now that there's no fences to hold them back?"

"I'm no cowboy, and neither are you. Besides, I need to stay closer to the city and I sold my stock. Things have been getting hairy out here."

"Tell you what, you bring that special thing we talked about it, with all of the toys that come with it, and I'll give you six does, a nice mature buck and two babies from other mothers. I'll take three guys work for a week and that sound fair?"

"You're serious? Three guys?"

Joe felt bad, he knew he was pushing the limits of friendship here, but Randy was city council in Brackettville and much better off than they were. That's why it puzzled him on why he'd wanted the animals so badly.

"Sure, three guys. Ones who can swing a hammer and help an old guy clean up some around the

40

THE WORLD ON FIRE

farm."

"If you're throwing in two young ones and a buck to boot, I think I'm getting the better part of a deal."

That gave him pause. Maybe he should push for more, but he looked at the inside of his cramped house.

"Naw, I just got room for three guys. How about you send me a bag of rice or something to even it out if it hurts your sense of fairness," Joe said, smiling at his joke.

Now he was playing with him, and he didn't tell him he was planning on sending Bucky, the goat from hell, father of half of the small herd of goats running around. He'd almost pay to have that goat gone.

"Ok, that sounds fair. Besides, these guys working for you will be doing some learning about taking care of these animals so don't feel bad. It's going to work for all of us. I'll have them bring the goats back when the time's up," Randy said, the radio crackling.

"Sounds like my batteries are about dead, Randy. Tomorrow sound good?"

"Sounds good to me. Over and out," Joe said, killing his radio.

Joe opened the battery compartment open and pulled the small battery bank out and started walking towards his barn where he had the small panel hidden. He got it out and laid things out to recharge the batteries in the cool shade. Since the power had gone out, Joe had taken to sleeping in the barn more than in his cinder block house. The barn was drafty, but in South Texas, it got hot in the summer time and in a world without air conditioning, a hammock in the barn was a good compromise for his weary bones.

§ § §

Joe slept hard, and when he woke, he wiped his face down and swung his legs off the hammock and grabbed his boots, shaking them first to make sure nothing had climbed in. He used to put the big Ziploc bags over the leg holes and use a rubber band to make sure no creepy crawlies got in there, but he found out it never let his boots dry out enough, or air out. Shaking and banging them together worked to get the blood flowing anyways. Stretching, he put his boots on and left the barn to run the old hand pump and check on his herd.

It was twilight, his favorite time of the day. Joe had gotten used to a 3rd shift existence on the police force. Out here, it was the quietest shift available, and it was always a lot cooler out of the sun. When the AC was no more, he'd started his old habit back up with more than a little ease. It made things harder when tending to his forty odd goats and assorted babies, but with the scorching summer temps, many of them hung out in the shade, venturing out in the dark hours as well.

"C'mere ya little punk," Joe said to an angry

THE WORLD ON FIRE

looking goat.

Bucky looked at Joe sullenly from behind the now useless hot wire and top strand of barbed wire. Joe knew he could get out of his own run, but hadn't for some reason. Maybe he was getting too old to get up to his usual shenanigans, Joe wondered then shook his head. Instead he took his pail to the hand pump and filled the bucket and walked it over to Bucky's pen.

"Here's a drink for ya, ya big baby," he said, rubbing the animal's head as he finally came closer to the topped off water trough.

"Yer going on now. Hope ya don't mind, but you're going to have a ton of fun annoying the hell out of my buddy Randy," he smiled and walked back to the hand pump and set up the downspout he'd pulled off an old tumble down shack for this purpose.

Once the power had gone out, he still had the hand pump that had been there since he was a kid and he'd rigged the solar pumps for the wells on the property, but by the barn, he pumped by hand. The long downspouts leaked a little bit when he had all the sections put together, but it was a better workaround than filling five or six buckets a few times a day. Joe pumped and the water started rushing down towards the paddock the does were in, separate from Bucky. Their trough was four to five times as big, but if he did this a couple of times a day, it wasn't hard to keep his small herd happy.

Smiling to himself, contemplating the repetitive life he'd had in the past two months, he was suddenly surprised to see a flash of light wink on in the distance through the scrub, and then wink out again. A cold shiver of fear worked its way through his body and he walked towards his house, pulling the keys out of his pocket. A few seconds later, he was walking into the explosive heat of the cinder block house and into his old bedroom. The smell almost always surprised him. The smell of humanity, of dirty clothes left to bake in the relentless heat. Quickly, Joe grabbed the gun from under his bed and pulled his pistol out and put it in a holster before putting that on as well.

"Hey, look at this!" Joe heard yelled from outside. Quietly, he worked his way out towards the darkened doorway and looked out.

A flashlight was playing its light across the paddock of goats and voices floated out of the darkness until he could see three shapes join whomever had the flashlight. Joe was careful not to look into the light too much and slipped out of the house and walked to his left without turning his body, keeping everything in sight. Bucky let out an alarmed bleat before a laugh came out of the dark. One of the figures tried climbing the wire fence but tripped, snagging in the top wire.

The curses weren't in English or Spanish. They were in an accent that Joe had only heard once before, at a conference in San Antonio. It'd be horrible of him to make an assumption, but this time of night, he was expecting to hear Spanish from

THE WORLD ON FIRE

'Coyotes' bringing people over… or home now that America had nothing left to offer. Arabic was the last thing he expected to hear.

Slinking through the shadows, Joe stepped into the darkened doorway of the barn, now directly across from the four or five men. He couldn't tell in the dark for sure, but when the man who fell on the fence started talking and gesturing loudly, and another pulled off a backpack and dug through it before handing something to him. The flashlight played over his hands and the fence for a moment, long enough for Joe to see the small bolt cutters part his barbed wire.

With only a flash to think, he considered just shooting the men, or at least one to make a point, but he didn't know how many of them were armed and how many were in the scrub across the street. Obviously they wanted the goat and weren't too concerned being quiet. If he shouted out a call or warning, he might make himself a target, but doing nothing was just getting him a cut fence and a stolen goat that was already promised out.

His rifle shot almost deafened him and the flash suppressor kept him from being completely blinded. He moved as fast as his body would let him out of the doorway and behind what he hoped would be a good spot behind a pile of pallets and shouted, "Police! Freeze!"

One man almost fell over backwards in surprise, two flinched at the sound of the shot but the last man he could see, turned towards him with his

BOYD CRAVEN

hands held at waist level pointing....

"Shit," Joe muttered quietly as the night was broken again by the sounds of gunfire.

The ground between the stack of pallets and the open barn door erupted into explosions of dust and dirt as rounds were hosed into where the shooter thought Joe was. The gunfire had an odd stuttering chatter, one that made his heart almost stop beating. The sound of an AK-47 was unmistakable to folks in the military or law enforcement, and on tilt, his beloved IMI Galil sounded much the same if bump fired, but it fired much different rounds than the little 7.62x39's the AK favored.

The other difference he saw as he peeked around the corner when the gunfire went silent was the shooter reloading. Coming to a kneeling position, Joe fired two shots center mass at the man. He flinched when the pallets started spraying him with wooden shrapnel as two more guns opened up.

"What the..."

A sharp sliver hit Joe in the face, right under his left eye and he cried out, dropping his gun for a moment, fearing for the loss of his eye. All coherent thought stopped as he pulled the nearly 2" long sliver out of his skin. It hadn't gone deep and was well under his eye and he almost missed hearing the footsteps over the constant gunfire. Grabbing his gun from the dirt he shook it to make sure nothing solid was lodged in the barrel and considered his options.

He was being pinned down behind a poor

46

THE WORLD ON FIRE

piece of cover and the men seemed to have started spreading out. Joe considered making a break for the barn when a man stumbled over a small scrub the goats had missed. Half a heartbeat to get the gunsight onto the dark figure in the dark. Half a heartbeat to ensure himself of the target and pull the trigger. The figure fell and, in an instant, Joe realized what had happened.

The men had been hosing the area with bullets, and if the gun flashes hadn't blinded them he would have been dead. Instead, the man missed a stupid little bush and stumbled, giving Joe time to put the bullet where it needed to go. Deciding to try his luck before Murphy of Murphy's Law showed up, he ran backwards towards the barn, expecting to feel the hot burn of a bullet in his back. Making it into the darkness surprised him, but he could hear two men conversing now.

He'd expected to hear Spanish earlier and had gotten Arabic, but now he was hearing a voice cursing someone named Rishaan in Spanish, and the unmistakable sound of a magazine change. Joe wedged himself back into the darkness until his bony ass found the edge of his workbench, an old solid piece of oak that used to be the front door of his parents' original house. It was old, weather beaten and a good place to hide and not expose himself to the front door. More shouts, more cursing.

"They must have found Rishaan," Joe thought to himself and waited.

What happened next wasn't what people would

think an honorable man would do, not one who was elected Sheriff of the county for many years until he retired to care after the goats and his small piece of heaven… but times had changed. Two figures stepped into the doorway, the scant moonlight silhouetting them walking in, rifles up to bear. Joe fired at center mass, two for each figure. One dropped and the other ran, stumbling.

"Oh shit," Joe told the darkened room when it became apparent that the threat was over.

A crushing pain started somewhere on his left side and Joe grabbed for the side of the bench as his feet went rubbery.

"That damn goat better stay in his pen," Joe panted.

CHAPTER 5

BRACKETTVILLE TEXAS – BRAD

Hot damn, but I was tired. The wind up alarm clock had been found, and it was now going off. Before it was even light out. We'd sat through the Mayor's radio conversation with a friend of his, a retired sheriff or chief or something. The job was going to be a piece of cake. We'd go there, help the old man fix things up, learn about the goats and how to milk them, and after a week we'd come home.

"Kill that thing," I heard from the other room.

Stuart hated mornings, especially now that he was back.

We had talked to the Mayor for a while last night. Stu was worried about not going and reporting in immediately, but without transportation, the closest military base was Laughlin Air Force Base, thirty miles away. I didn't have enough gas for a round trip, and the Mayor hadn't seemed inclined to help in that regard, even though there were plenty of vets and volunteers.

"We just lost too many people," he kept saying.

We'd also talked about the coming invasion. That seemed unreal. I mean, with the Air Force base in operation nearby, surely they'd pound any large force into the dirt.

"On it," I said, hitting it again and swinging my legs out of bed.

We'd negotiated with the Mayor for gas and food. Almost five gallons of gas for a week's worth of labor. It would be more than enough for me to get Stuart to the base and back, and then he wouldn't be worried about not reporting in as directed. Walking, it'd take him a few days.

"You going to bring your kit?" Stuart asked me, his voice floating out of the darkness.

My kit was modeled after his. It was an old framed Molle pack much like his was. I kept spare clothing, belt, socks and three one-liter canteens on it. Inside, he'd helped me put together a 'survival kit', in case of emergencies. I doubted I'd ever need half the stuff, having grown up playing in the scrub, but it made sense. I decided to add more ammo than I normally carried in case I got some hunting in while I was down there. Who knows, maybe I could bag a nice fat buck.

"Yeah," I said, already dressing for the day.

Lights filtered in through the bedroom as a

THE WORLD ON FIRE

pickup truck crunched the gravel of the drive-way, its headlights blinding me. I finished in half a heartbeat and slid my feet into my boots. It was hot already, and I knew it would only get worse. Nowhere near as bad as the dog days of summer, but I'd learned quickly that a life without air conditioning was something that took some adjusting to.

"C'mon man… he's here," Stuart yelled.

"I know," I grouched, grabbing my pack and my gun.

I'd added extra clothing and toiletries before falling asleep last night, so essentially I was ready. My gun, besides the 1911, was an old SKS. Ammo was easy to find, cheap and, if I wrecked it, I literally had three spares in the safe. I just had to trust Randolph's word that everything in the house would be looked after and safe from looters while we were gone… that was the one thing that had really bugged me.

A horn honked just as I made it out the front door and I turned to lock it. It was a very quick muted beep, one probably designed to hurry me up but not wake all the neighbors. I ignored everyone and did both the handle lock and the deadbolt, knowing that it wasn't that much of a deterrent when sheets of glass could be gone through easily. I was probably paranoid but I didn't care. I tossed my pack into the bed of the old Chevy that looked like it'd been put back together with duct tape and bailing wire. Despite that, I could hear the motor humming in perfect tune.

51

BOYD CRAVEN

"Let's go ladies, I have to go pick up Spencer on our way out to Spafford," Randolph said, a grin on his face.

"Is that coffee I smell?" I asked, pushing Stuart to the middle next to the Mayor.

"Sorta, smells and tastes like it but it's more of a tea…" Randolph paused and handed a thermos over to us, "It's roasted mesquite pods. Make it every year for my parents… except… well, I still made it this year."

I nodded silently; we'd all lost someone.

"So wait, that's from those seeds? We just threw them out when they fell to the lawn," Stuart said.

"Yeah, you pick them sometime in July or August when the pods turn tan or a white color. Bust them up into two-inch chunks. Then you roast them over low heat like you would a cake and when they are dried out, you can grind them up and cook it like cowboy coffee."

"Your wife's percolator?" I asked him.

"Smart aleck, yeah, a percolator. Cowboy coffee. Come on, we're guys, this is a guy thing. You really didn't know that? Yer a Texan, aren't ya?" His tone was teasing, but his eyes never left the road.

"I know that the critters like it sometimes," I admitted, "But I've always been more into the… meat group side of things." I told them.

"Just like I'm into the shooting and blowing up things?" Stu said, grinning.

"Something like that," I agreed.

"You two should keep all the pods you find next

52

THE WORLD ON FIRE

year. You can grind the seeds and make a kinda flour meal, or just eat them. Lots of good things come from the regular plants around here."

"Just like they taught us in SERE," Stuart tells me with a grin, "if it's good enough for the animals, it's probably good enough for us."

"You can eat your worms and berries, I'd rather have a steak," I told them grinning, watching the landscape change as we approached the outer edge of the county.

I knew we were going to pick up Spencer, but the truck had one long bench seat. One of us was going to have to ride in the back and I liked my kidneys, so I hoped the younger man didn't mind it too much. As it turns out, he didn't. He had a pack of his own and made himself a comfortable spot and tipped his hat low before we pulled out. He would probably be asleep by the time we got there. Listening to Stuart and Randolph talk, I leaned against the glass and drifted off.

§ § §

"Something's wrong, hey..." Stuart's voice broke through, interrupting my dream as he nudged me awake with his shoulder.

"What?" I asked sitting up.

The truck had stopped, but we weren't parked in any driveway. I felt the truck shift as Spencer hopped out somewhere behind me. I knew that because he was opening the door I was leaning on

53

and…

"Shit," I mumbled, almost falling on my head.

I was saved that embarrassment by Stuart grabbing me. I got out and looked around. Cars that had stalled and left, lined the highway here and there. The dust covering the windshields almost made them dark inside, but it wasn't the stalled cars that the three of them were looking at… It was the birds circling the sky. Carrion birds.

"Where are we?" I ask them.

"Half a mile from Joe's place. There's too many of them for it to be from him processing a goat. Something's wrong," Randy said.

"How'd you even see them? The sun's barely up."

"Isn't a lot else to look at out here. Was picking my way through the road and saw a slow moving cloud. Turned out to be crows or some such. You ever seen something like this?" he asked me.

I nodded, "Yeah, when I make a lot of kills on a farm somewhere. Unless they're paying me to dispose of the hogs, I just leave them in a pile or row. That's why I love shooting from my fourwheeler. At the end of the trip I just drag them off with a tow strap."

The Mayor nodded.

"So what's been dragged into a pile there?" he asked no one, then reached behind his seat and grabbed his rifle.

I grabbed my backpack, and got my rifle out of the back of the truck as well.

"Let's go in quiet," Stuart said.

THE WORLD ON FIRE

We all nodded and followed him. He hadn't brought a rifle, but he did have his .44, and he pulled that out of the holster. Randy and I were both holding guns, but seeing Stuart un-nerved enough to draw his put me on edge. His whole body language had changed as well. He moved with purpose, and I followed him. Behind me, Randolph and Spencer tried to emulate his body language.

Fear, real fear, made my adrenaline soar. It does funny things to your body. Your senses get cranked up past the normal levels, and it becomes hard not to get tunnel vision. I'd had that happen to me on several hunts where a wild boar I'd shot turned and charged. This was different. I'd been on enough hunts with Stuart that I recognized when he put his hand up into a fist that it meant stop. I slid behind some scrub on the edge of the road and peered around and watched him move from cover to cover.

It wasn't long and he was back, the color drained out of his face.

"We've got a problem," he whispered when the four of us were all together again.

"What's going on?" Spencer asked quietly.

"In the yard, there's four or five dead tangos. Looks like a hell of a gunfight happened," Stu told us, his voice quiet.

"Is Joe…?" Randolph asked.

"I don't know. I… I didn't see him. Other than the goats, it looks like there's no movement," Stu said, his words sinking in, making Randolph wince.

"Let's go check it out," I said, surprising everyone.

"What?" Spencer asked.

"The die-off happened everywhere. If something happened, there's bound to be people who heard it here in town…"

"Dude, this is like the world's smallest small town ever." Stu said.

"I still need to check on Joe," Randolph said.

"We will. Spencer and Randolph, cover Brad and I at the fences, that way if we need to leave in a hurry…"

"Got it," Spencer said and Randolph nodded.

I had done it enough in game drives with Stuart, and we spread out by five or six yards and slowly advanced on the farm. His handgun was out, ready to use and I made sure my SKS was still ready to roll. The first thing I noticed was the smell. The heat hadn't really kicked all the way in, but already, I could smell the goats and their enclosure. It doesn't matter how clean you keep farm animals, they are still farm animals and each has its on odor. This wasn't horrible, but there was something else in the air and I didn't like it.

I could smell something coppery, overlaid with something much worse. The goats made noises, and I went in through the front gate, joined by Stu a second later. The farm was laid out in what looked like a haphazard pattern of small outbuildings and fences. The house was made of cement block, and the barn looked old and ready to fall down. I know

THE WORLD ON FIRE

looks can be deceiving, but out here, when something sits in the sun and bakes for fifty years, it all starts to look washed out, dried up and ready to…

"Look alive," Stu said pointing.

Two dead men were laid out on the ground. One had died on his side, the other face down. Their features were dark and I covered Stu with the rifle while he went and checked each of them for a pulse. I could smell the voided bowels and shuddered. Hunting animals was one thing, but I don't think I could ever do what Stuart did for the Army, I didn't think I could take a life. I saw two forms in the open doorway of the barn, arms and legs akimbo and pointed with my right hand when he was done looking at the dead men on the ground.

He followed my hand with his eyes and nodded. When he stood, his knees popped, the loudest thing I ever heard it seemed, and my heart started thundering, making it hard to listen to everything else. He walked slowly to the barn, not taking cover as he went, just walking slowly, heel to toe, not making much noise. He used his foot to kick away the guns near the dead men, and headed into the darkness.

"Stay there," he said.

I reached down and grabbed one of the guns and immediately realized what it was. It was an AK-47, something that shot the same ammunition as my SKS. I used to own one, but when I checked closer I realized that it wasn't the same gun you could find in gun shops all over the country. The wood on the

57

stock looked kind of orange and the grip almost felt greasy. I put the SKS over my shoulder and held the AK up and smelled it. It still had the packing grease on it in some areas.

I felt the dead man's pockets with dread, but found nothing. He had a small pack and I pulled that loose. A few bottles of water and some spare magazines already loaded were the only thing inside of it. I moved on to the second dead man and checked him for weapons or traps, and I could hear Stuart inside the barn moving around. My eyes were starting to adjust to the gloomy interior and I could make out his shape as he went through it. The second man's pack held much of the same. I almost missed something with the second body and stood up and looked.

Their skin tone was a little darker than mine, but that had always seemed par for the course down here where Hispanic and Native blood was involved, but it was their features that gave me pause. I leaned the AKs on the wall outside he barn and gave a short whistle. When Stuart didn't respond, I walked in.

"He's over here." Stuart's voice floated out from a dark corner and I followed it until I saw him kneeling down, feeling for a pulse on an inert body. It must be Joe.

"Is he hit?" I asked him.

"No, but he's dead," Stuart told me.

"How?" I asked him, feeling confused and nervous.

THE WORLD ON FIRE

"He's clutching his left side. If I had to guess, he had a heart attack after the shoot 'em up."

I looked him over, and couldn't see anything wrong, but the older man looked gray in the gloom, probably a side effect of the lighting.

"He's got an AK also?" I asked, picking a gun up from the work bench he'd collapsed near.

"Think that's something else. Looks like a Galil. It's like an AK but shoots a .308," Stu told me.

"Huh. I wonder why he wanted that sharpshooters gun then? I mean, that's one of the trade items on the list…"

"I have no idea. I'm just trying to figure out why a coyote was with these guys. Lately traffic seems to go south across the border, but I doubt these guys were traveling south."

"You noticed the men aren't all Mexican then?" I asked him, that still worrying me.

"Yeah, I can't pin country of origin down, but these guys are not from here. I'd say they're recently off the boat from somewhere. Maybe a forward recon group?"

"Dude, maybe you're paranoid," I told him.

"Hey, you guys all right?!" The shout startled me, but Stu put a hand up on my shoulder to steady me.

Spencer and Randolph were crossing into the farm through the same gate we did. Randolph had his gun up on the ready and Spencer looked around nervously. Stu walked out into the light and headed to meet them.

BOYD CRAVEN

"Sorry about this, Joe," I said reaching for his pockets, "But I have to check you over, man. The world has gone all crazy, and I don't know if you have any family or not but if you don't... There's a lot of people who could benefit from anything you have or don't have. I mean, you may not need it anymore. I'm sure Randolph will have a proper funeral. I just really wish you could tell me what the hell happened here."

Of course he didn't say anything, but I felt guilty rifling through the pockets of a dead man. I looked up to see the three of them examining the bodies that were in the middle of the farm yard. Truth was, when everything ended, the trucks stopped running. Food quit getting delivered. If we hadn't figured out how to purify our water, we'd have risked getting sick. For us, boiling the water meant that we had to find something to make a fire with, and after a couple months of constantly needing to do it, we were running out of anything coming close to dried wood. Even the mesquite tree we'd talked about had been chopped down.

The only thing I found of any note was a set of keys. Probably to the house and a car by the look of it. I hadn't seen a car. I stood and stretched, hoping my hammering heart would slow down a bit so I didn't feel like I was running a marathon. I slowly walked through the barn and found a pallet of bagged feed for the goats and a funny looking stand that had a V shape and two pails next to it. I went over to look and almost tripped over a stool.

THE WORLD ON FIRE

A milking stand if I had to guess, but I'd have to ask Randolph if I really wanted to know.

"You ok in there?" Stu yelled.

"Yeah, just checking stuff out." I called back.

"Oh man, Joe," Randolph said, walking towards his friend's crumpled form.

I kept going past what I had decided was a milking stand and towards a blue tarped shape in the corner. I pulled on the edge of the tarp and a late 70s car sat there, a little dusty, but pretty good looking considering everything.

"That's his pride and joy," Randolph said from somewhere behind me.

"Does it go fast?" I asked him without looking.

"Should. He had the motor rebuilt when he got the car."

"Does he have any family?" I ask, already wondering what was going to happen.

I hated to sound like a creepy looter, but the guy had lots of food on the hoof, with the ability to also have milk and cheese, running water... I felt embarrassed by the way my mind was wandering, but in part this was what Randolph was going to set up for the town.

"Not anymore," Randolph said, "Not that I know of. Shit. We've got to report this, but I'm not going to leave Joe here for the buzzards."

"I'll help dig," Spencer offered from the open door.

"Yeah, we'll have to take turns. The ground is going to be hard pack."

"Probably easier in the garden. It's just behind his house. I guess he said this year's garden didn't do too bad."

"Garden?" Both Stu and I chorused from different sides of the Mayor.

"Yeah, let's go look."

CHAPTER 6

They had been on the road for three days. While they'd been stopped, their APC had had maintenance done by Silverman's Militia/Reserve team who was handling a second training facility. With winter almost upon them, every Mechanic who could, was being pressed into service getting vehicles and machinery ready for the fight that was fixing to spill into the southern states and move up the country.

"Seems to run better," Michael said.

"Purrs," King agreed.

Michael had shown King how to operate the controls on the APC, something he was vaguely familiar with, and he'd been driving for the day. They had gone silent today, turning their radios off. They hadn't slowed down through the areas they had

63

cleared. Instead, they alternated driving and only took meal and restroom breaks. One would drive, one would sleep. Even though they'd traveled much of the same roads to head back towards Louisiana, they were soon going to stash the APC and go in via truck.

"Your turn?" King asked.

"I don't mind," Michael said, trading seats with him.

King stood and stretched and pulled the map out and used a penlight to consult it.

"We want to be quiet when we get close," King said, "Not even alert the Guard as we roll through an area."

"When do you think we're going to stash the APC?" Michael asked.

"Tomorrow."

§ § §

It had been getting cooler in Kentucky, but when they stashed the APC, it was hot in Texas. They found an abandoned auto shop with cinderblock walls and a deep, almost warehouse-like building connected to it. They stashed it in the back and tarped the front of the APC so even a casual look inside a window would just show a dark bay and an even darker warehouse. It'd already been stripped of anything of use, and the town was dead, literally dead. Both streets coming and going lead to and from Brackettville.

64

THE WORLD ON FIRE

"Why not stash it closer to a bigger town?" Michael asked.

"Would you remember if two dudes drove in with that?"

"Well… Yeah," Michael admitted.

"Once we get closer," King said, "We become ghosts."

"Where are we crossing into Mexico, exactly?" Michael asked as they grabbed their gear and checked their laces.

"Jimenez," King said, walking now.

Michael followed. "Ok. How far till the next big town?"

"If you start saying 'are we there yet?' it's going to be time for more PT," King grumbled.

"No, I mean, a couple weeks? Days?"

"Days," King said, adjusting the straps on his pack as he walked.

They'd both been given new packs with camelbacks for water. Michael wasn't carrying a heavy load out like King was, his pack mostly consisted of the basics. They had planned on doing what he had been doing in the national forest when they weren't traveling and blowing stuff up; they would be living off the land once their MREs from Sandra had run out, and they'd head north to resupply when they could get secure communications established.

§ § §

They found a broken down car to use as a wind-

65

break and went to sleep with no fire. It got cold at night, but not horribly.

"Next time maybe we should sleep in the car," Michael grouched as he got up.

"Up to you," King said.

They set out after changing out their socks and kept going before the heat of the sun. Slowly their muscles loosened up and the soreness left Michael's body. He was feeling pretty good when King stiffened and stopped. He pulled his binoculars up and looked in the direction King was looking and saw what looked like a ring of cars in the median. Smoke drifted up lazily from a still lit campfire. Adjusting the focus, Michael saw a ring of men sleeping. He handed the binoculars to King who took a look.

"Thirteen. I see beer cans and trash everywhere. Guns. No Hispanics, no blacks."

"That doesn't mean anything, does it?" Michael asked.

"Black man in the deep South, you get a feel for things. I think that's trouble."

They both crouched down and Michael pulled out his map. They were studying for a moment and then made a plan. It worked for the most part. They walked for an hour straight east, and then using the compass, they walked south, paralleling the road. They both sweated and ached. The sun was coming up and the heat of the day was about to hit them.

"Glass a shady spot," King said, pulling the vest and backpack off on their break.

Michael did the same and got his binoculars

66

THE WORLD ON FIRE

out again. Much of the area was just desert. Scrub and small brush hung close to the ground in places; finding water was going to be one of the next problems to address.

"There," Michael said pointing slightly to the south west, "It's getting close to the road again, but I can make out a big rock outcropping. If we put up a tarp we should be able to get some shade.

"Lead on," King said smiling as Michael put the map and compass away.

He'd been teaching the kid some hands-on things. Reading the map, accounting for compass declination. Navigating with his wits and very simple tools. Not that a GPS wouldn't have been a fun toy for Sandra to have included. The one in the APC wasn't portable, so they were doing it the old way.

"Do you think we're far enough past that camp to go there?" Michael asked.

"Depends if it was a camp or an outpost," King said.

"Oh, I'll keep my eyes out."

King smiled, he would too and he just nodded and started putting his gear back on. After taking a hit of water, they both started walking again. After another thirty minutes, they were able to reach the outcropping and set up a crude quick shelter and they settled to rest underneath it. King looked at the map and pointed to the spot they were at.

"We're closer than I thought," Michael told him.

"Brackettville by the afternoon," King told him.

"I wonder how many people are still alive there,"

he said softly.

"There's not many people left anywhere. Things are bad, and they're about to be worse."

Michael nodded and pulled his shirt off and used it as a mat and laid his back down on it, letting the sparse wind cool him.

"What was Sandra like?" Michael asked suddenly.

"When?" King asked.

"When you trained her. I didn't think they let girls into combat roles until a year or two ago?"

"She wasn't exactly normal military," King said.

"CIA?" Michael asked, suddenly not as sleepy as he thought.

"Different alphabet, same sort of game," King admitted, his white teeth flashing in a rare grin.

"You were too then... I'm just curious. It's like you're some beefed up James Bond and she's the size... I mean, she's like... My old girlfriend's size."

"You should know better," King said, "Size doesn't make a difference. Girl was 19 when they sent her to me. She was smart. Tough. Prayed. I think she had God on her side, but I don't know much about that. She was good, learned quick. Smart."

"You loved her?" Michael asked.

"In a way. Like a daughter," he admitted.

Michael nodded in understanding. He didn't know the age of the big man, but he was guessing that King was older than he looked.

"Am I ever going to be that good?" Michael

asked.

"I hope you never have to be."

Michael chewed on that for a moment, "You keep teaching me things. Is this part of the training?" he asked.

"You stop learning, you start dying," King said and rolled onto his side.

Before Michael could respond, the larger man started snoring softly.

"I wish I could do that," Michael said, rolling onto his back again.

CHAPTER 7

SAUZ, MEXICO –
THE NEW CALIPHATE

I am missing Rishaan's report," Khalid told his subordinate.

"He has not radioed back in," he was told.

"Find out; I don't want to send a small force to the auxiliary airport if I do not have to," he snarled.

"Yes, of course," the other man replied, before turning to leave.

Their main objective had been met months ago, when what was supposed to have been a satellite launch had in fact been a joint effort between the New Caliphate and North Korea – who supplied the material and equipment – to detonate a nuclear reaction above the United States. They believed that they had done what no other country or nation had ever done: utterly defeat and annihilate a government without suffering losses themselves.

THE WORLD ON FIRE

They'd let the Americans throw away their lives, overextending the military, making them spend money they didn't have… wasting lives. They did not understand that not all wars were fought the way they had been. Khalid Abdul was born to parents who had been killed by weapons that the Americans had supplied to various factions around the Middle East and he'd been raised on the run, from one government or another, by his great uncle. He'd fought in Afghanistan and was heading to Syria when he was called to change his plans and fulfill his lifelong dream.

Revenge. Power. He wasn't a religious man himself, not like the Caliphate's leader, but to admit that would be literal suicide considering the company he kept. He prayed like everyone else, knew what to say and when to say it, but a lifetime of horrors had steeled his heart against any sort of faith. Revenge and power fueled him; that was his course and that was his religion. One of his most trusted scouts, Rishaan, had been sent out three days ago to scout the Laughlin Air Force Base's auxiliary airport.

His job was to have been simple: scout the area to make sure it was a backup landing strip. The aerial photography he got made it look as if it was just that's all it was. If that was the case, the main attacking force would be centered on the main base north of there. His attack would be the first overt move against the government he hated. The government that supplied weapons and money, corrupting men's minds with their lies. The other commanders

71

had done smaller invasions throughout the south-west United States, but the reason his men called him the 'Spear of Allah', was because he planned to strike at the heart of the country.

"Sir," the man was back, "Rishaan cannot be raised. He is not transmitting—"

"Or he's dead," Khalid said, "Very well. I want two squads to head to this location where Khalid must have been and—"

"His radio beacon is still active, and they say it hasn't moved."

"What?" Khalid asked.

"So we could track his progress; his radio has a GPS chip in it. It hasn't moved since last night. He's a little north of the location he was to have scouted."

"And you say it hasn't moved?" Khalid asked.

"No."

"Then he is dead. Send four squads to that location and, once secured, have them join in the main attacking force at Laughlin."

"Yes, Khalid," the man said, ducking back out of the tent.

Khalid smiled. Tonight, America would tremble in fear.

CHAPTER 8

SPAFFORD TEXAS – BRAD

Digging is hard work. I much prefer hunting to digging, but we found the ground by the garden to be easy to dig until we got to the hard pack about thirty inches in. Spencer took over for a while with a pickaxe he found in the barn and we alternated until we had enough space dug to bury Joe properly. Stu finished the filling in while Randolph was inspecting all the weapons, after dumping the four bodies in the desert.

"Now what?" I asked Randolph, knowing the job was now over.

"I hate to say it, but I guess we gather everything up that isn't nailed down. Joe doesn't have any kin close to here, and we've been horse trading forever. I'll store his stuff till the—"

"Excuse me, mister?" A small, quiet voice called

out, making us all turn.

There was a young girl, probably no more than seven or eight years old, carrying a glass jug. She looked thin, but healthy. Her brown eyes were staring holes into me.

"Yes ma'am? How can I help you," I asked her.

"Is Mister Joe going to be milking today? Momma's sick and she couldn't walk over here herself."

We shot pained looks back and forth until everyone looked at me. Great.

"Mr. Joe had a run in with some folks, and he passed away," I explained to her.

"He was shot?" she asked, alarmed.

"No, I think he had a heart attack from all the action," I told her, "Do you normally get milk from him?" I asked.

"Yes sir. We also make the cheese. It isn't the hard kind like the store, but it spreads good. Other than the tortillas and lizards, it's the only food we got."

Randolph made a choking sound and I looked up to see him wiping a piece of grit out of his eyes, either that or the wiry Texan was starting to get choked up.

"I don't know how to milk a goat. Does anybody here know how?" I asked and everyone shook their heads no, "Do you know how to?" I asked her.

"I tried to help once, but I got scared. I've watched him plenty of times," she told me.

"If you can walk me through it, maybe I'll give it a shot?" I asked her, and for the first time she

THE WORLD ON FIRE

smiled.

"Mommy doesn't let me talk to strangers, but she's sick and I missed coming over yesterday. You won't tell her, will you?"

"Tell you what, my name is Brad Palmer. How about we go check on your momma and ask her if it's ok if you show me how to milk a goat?" I asked her.

"She's sick though. You might catch what she's got," she shot right back.

"Well, how about your daddy?" I asked her. "He wouldn't let his daughter talk to strangers. Besides, I bet I might have something in my backpack that would make your mommy feel better. Medicines?"

"Dude…." Stu said, but I waved him off.

"Ok, well… My name is Maria, and my mom's Marcy. Daddy died when I was a baby."

"Well, it's nice to meet you Maria; let me go get my bag."

She watched me with big eyes as I pulled out a small red bag that had a flap that rolled it shut, making it mostly waterproof. It was my first aid kit, something I always kept handy, especially when out in the middle of nowhere. Hunting hogs can get a bit dangerous, and getting gashed or gored by their tusks was always on my big list of what not to have happen, so I kept more than the usual Band-Aids; I'd thrown in some antibiotics I'd purchased online. I had a hundred capsules each of amoxicillin, and Keflex, all available over the counter for use in your fish tank.

It was even the same formula and dosages that humans used. I'd learned about it on the Doom and Bloom blog back before the world had ended with an EMP, erasing everything.

"Do you want a hand?" Randolph asked.

"I got this," I told him.

The girl seemed skittish, but I was probably the least threatening-looking of the group. I followed her across the street and up about a block. We passed a few houses and it was heart-breakingly evident that it hadn't been an affluent neighborhood, even before the EMP. One of the houses we passed, the curtains were moved and then fell back into place, making me wonder how many people were around, how many people might be shut inside watching. Maybe with rifles pointed at my back....

"You look like you're sick," she told me, "are you ok, mister?" Maria asked me.

"Oh, I'm ok," I reassured her. "Which house is yours?"

"The red one."

The red one it was. It was the nicer house on the street. The dark red probably didn't do much for keeping the house cool, and I wasn't surprised to see two AC units sitting side by side. The house wasn't large, but it had been built within the last ten years; the only structure in Spafford that could lay claim to that title by the look of things. Maria walked up to the front door and just pushed it open. I guess crime wasn't normally a big issue.

The smell hit me immediately. It smelled like an

THE WORLD ON FIRE

overflowing trashcan of dirty diapers.

"Maria," a weak voice called out.

"Be right there," she said, kicking her shoes off by the door.

Little things I noticed immediately. The house was spotless. It had recently been dusted and it was tastefully decorated with a southwest theme that was somewhat typical of where we live.

"Who's with you, baby?" a woman's voice said from a doorway we'd just walked past.

I stopped startled and turned. I don't know who was surprised more, me or the woman. She was surprisingly tall. You could tell that she'd been an absolute knockout, but either hunger or sickness had left her thin and hollow eyed.

"Who's this, Maria?" she asked, swaying on her feet.

"This is Brad, he's got medicine. He said he can help."

"You stay away from my daughter, you sick…"

I caught her as she slumped, and lowered her to the ground.

"Maria, go out the door and call for Stu, he's my friend. He'll come running."

"Is my mom going to be ok?"

"I think so," I told her.

I felt her forehead and she was burning up. I put my arms under her as Maria ran to the front door, screaming for my buddy, and scooped her mother up. She'd been coming out of a bathroom, evidently the source of the house's smell. The toilet wasn't

77

overflowing, but it wasn't pleasant. I made a mental note to get buckets of water from the old sheriff's house and flush it somehow. I went down the hallway, the woman light in my arms, and pushed open a door with my foot. The bedroom was painted pink and stickers adorned the wall and ceiling. Dora and Boots from Dora the Explorer. Those neon glow in the dark stars were stuck to the ceiling everywhere.

I went and pushed the next door open and saw I'd found the right room. A bucket had been placed near the bed. Mercifully, it was empty. Her four poster was high up enough I had to pull Marcy close to me and higher to get her onto it. I didn't bother covering her up; she felt warm. Warm and dry. That's when I started to worry. Marcy laid there limp and completely out of it.

"He's coming Mr. Brad," Maria said, standing in her mother's doorway.

"Get me a washcloth sweetheart," I called.

I kept a water bottle clipped to my belt and it had been lukewarm earlier, but it had cooled. I'd topped it off at Joe's hand pumped well during one of my digging breaks. I uncapped it and tried to pour a little over Marcy's chapped lips. She moaned and turned to the side.

"Here you go. Did she fall asleep again?" Maria asked, "She falls down and goes to sleep when it's really bad."

"How long has it been since she's eaten or drank anything?" I asked.

"Not today or yesterday. I think she was throw-

THE WORLD ON FIRE

ing up the day before. Two or three days, I think? Is my mommy going to be ok?"

"I think so, trust me. I'll do everything I can to help her," I told her, taking the washcloth and tousling her hair the way I'd seen people do to kids on TV.

I was trying to reassure her, but her mother wasn't sweating and that was a big sign of dehydration, heat stroke or heat exhaustion. She'd probably had a bad stomach bug, food poisoning or drank bad water and got sucked into a vicious cycle. I'd been there once. It hadn't been pleasant. I'd overdone it on a hunt and, when I collapsed, it had taken an IV bag of fluids to make me feel halfway human again. Throwing up, diarrhea and everything else had plagued me that day.

Cupping the washcloth in one hand, I wet it down with the water and press it onto her forehead. Marcy stretched and moaned. Rivulets of water from the damp cool cloth ran down the side of her face and she wiggled back and forth a bit, her eyes starting to flutter.

"Do you have any straws?" I asked Marcy.

"Yes, in the kitchen."

"Get me some."

She hurried off and Marcy opened her eyes and looked at me.

"If you hurt my daughter, I'll kill you," she whispered.

I smiled and sat on the edge of the bed, using my free hand to push the hair out of her eyes.

BOYD CRAVEN

"What are you doing?" she asked me.

"Your daughter found us to help. I promise, I'm not here to hurt you or her."

"Mommy!" Maria cried, jumping on the bed, a handful of plastic disposable straws in her hand.

She'd gone fast enough that I didn't expect her back so quickly.

"Here you go, Mister Brad." She held a pink and white striped plastic straw out to me.

I put it in the water bottle, pulled on the end and tilted it 90 degrees. When I held it up to Marcy, she turned to look at her daughter. Maria smiled back, happy to see her mother awake, I imagined. Then her eyes turned to me.

"Thank you," she said, and took a sip.

She must have been really dry, because the first sip had her coughing and gasping. I got the bucket and put it up. She held onto one side weakly and just shook her head at me.

"Brad?" I heard Stu yell from the front of the house.

"Back here, last door in the hallway."

Marcy's cough subsided and I handed her the water bottle.

"Take slow sips, or you're going to throw up," I told her.

Marcy nodded. I could tell she was swallowing a little fast, but I didn't stop her. I had collapsed once and immediately had gotten help, but she had been like this for a day or two... I was surprised she was ok.

80

THE WORLD ON FIRE

"Oh man," Stu said coming into the room, "What can I help with?" he said looking around.

"First things first, I need four or five buckets of water from the Sherriff's pump to get dumped down the bathroom toilet. She's been sick and I'm guessing she hasn't been able to haul water."

"No," Marcy said in a weak voice and then put her free hand on her stomach.

"Don't drink so fast, you'll cramp up," I told her.

"Sorry, I…"

She started heaving and I pulled the water bottle clear and made sure the bucket was close at hand. It was close, but she held everything down. She motioned for the water bottle, but I shook my head.

"You have to go slow," I told her, "You're badly dehydrated. Every time you throw up or use the restroom, you're making it worse. Trust me. Slow, and in a couple minutes we'll be able to get you more."

"My mouth is so dry," she rasped.

I pulled the washcloth down, and she pushed it against her lips. I could hear her sucking.

"Is there anyone here to take care of you?" I asked her.

"Man, what are you doing?" Stu, I'd forgotten about him.

"Stu, can you get those buckets of water for me?" I asked him again.

"Is she ok?" he asked.

"She should be. If you can do those buckets though, maybe use the truck and bring a bunch… I want to get the bathroom ready in case she has to

81

use it once we get some water in her."

"Ok, need anybody else?" he asked.

"No, just some bottles of water, buckets for the bathroom and my big pack. I've got some packets of Gatorade in there."

"You got it," he said and left.

Something had made him stop, hesitate. He was the soldier and he was used to action and orders. I smiled, it was something to razz him about later on. The washcloth was placed back on her head and she looked at me.

"What day is it?" she asked me.

"I don't keep track of that much," I told her.

Not that it was necessarily true, but my mind had been thrown for a loop somehow and I couldn't remember the date or the day of the week.

"How long have I been," she paused and looked at her daughter and then back at me, "out of it?"

I leaned in close and brushed the hair out of her face. She flinched back from having a stranger so close, but I was looking at her eyes. They'd been bloodshot. Probably from her throwing up. Petechia, I thought it's called.

"Just looking at your eyes."

"Why?" Her voice rasped again so I gave her the water bottle back. "Slow sips,"

She took two sips and pulled it away.

"How long?"

"Part of today, maybe some yesterday, according to Maria."

Marcy looked at her daughter and smiled.

THE WORLD ON FIRE

"Why are you here again?" she asked.

"Your daughter found us, asked us to help."

"No, why are you in Spafford? This isn't exactly a place people come to visit."

She took another sip, her voice cracking.

"We were going to visit Joe Green," I told her.

"Where?" she asked.

"He got into a gunfight with some..." I fought for the right words.

I'm not a racist, and I would never want to be labeled as such... But half everyone down this far south was of Mexican heritage and if I said Mexican as a white white guy, then I'd be called a racist. I didn't want to give that impression to a sick woman and her daughter who were definitely of Hispanic descent...

"A coyote was bringing some bad guys up across the border. I think they crossed Joe somehow."

"Oh no, is he dead?"

I just nodded gravely and, as dehydrated as she was, a single tear rolled down her cheek. I looked away and stood.

"I'll be right back, I'm going to check and see if..."

"It's me," Stu yelled and I walked to the front door to greet him.

"How'd you do that so fast?" I asked him.

"If it's for flushing, I got it out of the goats' water trough. We'll pump them some more. I got more buckets man," he said, passing me the handle and he walked back to the truck.

BOYD CRAVEN

The toilet wasn't plugged and it wasn't as bad as I thought it would be. It took two buckets of water and we refilled the bowl and then the top up as well. I walked out with the last empty bucket and got my pack out of the truck. Two full buckets were left so I just put them by the front porch and headed inside with my backpack.

"I'm sorry to be so much trouble," Marcy said, "if you have things to do…"

"Ma'am," I said, "I'll leave if you're uncomfortable, but you can barely get out of bed. All I've done is gotten half a liter of water into you. If I left now and something happened…" I looked over to Maria, "There's only a few people left around here, aren't there?"

"This isn't a place where people flee the cities to come visit," she said, her eyes getting heavy.

"Don't go to sleep just yet," I told her.

I had a store bought bottle of water, something that become rare. I opened the cap and then took out a plastic pack of Gatorade from my pack, added it in and shook it up. I handed it to her with a straw.

She struggled with the cap, proving my point she should not be left alone yet, so I took it back and opened it, putting her straw in. She took a sip and her eyes shot up.

"Oh God, I forgot how good sugar tastes." Marcy told me, her eyes wide.

"Sugar and salt, plus I think that one's orange flavored."

Her eyes locked onto mine and she took an-

84

other sip.

"Now, I've got some fixings here in my bag. You mind if I get something going for dinner?" I asked her.

"I haven't… I don't have much…"

"That's ok, I brought some."

The stove was an electric and, despite the lack of running water and electricity, the kitchen was very clean. I took my bag and headed that direction, and paused to talk to Maria.

"Hey, don't let your mom gulp that all at once. Ok?"

"I won't," she said, walking over to the side of the bed where I'd been standing moments before.

"No Mom, Mr. Brad said…"

I walked out of the room and headed towards the kitchen where I found Stu.

"Dude," he said quietly, sitting at a bar stool and a small breakfast nook island-y thing.

"Hey man," I told him.

"You really fixing to play Betty Crocker?" he asked.

"I don't know what I'm doing," I admitted, "I don't know what we're doing. I mean, the whole job's gone off the rails at this point. I don't know what Randolph is going to do."

"He's milking the goats, last I saw."

"What?" I asked, shocked.

"Found an old book in the barn. Must have shown it to the kid," he said, nodding back towards the bedroom.

"That's good then. I guess I've seen it on TV and could have figured it out but…"

"Why here? Is it the mom?" Stu asked me.

I stopped and stared at him. "What?"

"I've never seen you treat a lady so… tenderly? I know I've been gone for a while man, but you being in the same house with a single mom and her kid… the old Brad would have run screaming."

I rubbed my hands through my hair and then opened my bug out bag and got out my mini cooker. It was something I'd built myself using a coffee can and smaller sterno cans full of rubbing alcohol and toilet paper to use as a wick. It wouldn't bring things up to a hard boil, but it would make it hot enough to dissolve seasonings or make coffee. I'd have to use more of a fire or modify things to make it able to active boil water I guess. But for heating water for some packages of Mountain House, it was good.

"The mom is in pretty desperate shape. Trust me, it's not anything like romance."

"Huh. Then why?"

Why? I really wanted to know myself. I'm not a jerk, but this was a bit out of character even for me and it had been obvious to Stu right away. The old me would have just given her a few bottles of water, gave the kid some rations and split like an hour ago. Running.

"The kid has no one else. If her mom dies…"

"So you're here in case the mom dies and you adopt the daughter?"

THE WORLD ON FIRE

"No, it's not like that… Screw you," I said, filling my pot with three bottles of water and lighting the sterno can.

"Dude… Don't get defensive. Besides, you might freak out the kid."

"Hey soldier boy, how about you backtrack and see where that coyote and his three compadres came in from?"

"Uh huh. Going to get rid of me quickly, eh?"

"Yeah, probably. I don't know, man. You're putting me on the spot and I don't know why I'm not being me. So instead of me working out why, you're needling me about it and I just want to help them and…"

"And what?" he asked, all teasing out of his voice.

"I don't know. I guess become a goat farmer back in town."

"This town?" he asked, his eyebrows raised comically.

"No, by our house," I told him.

"Ahhhh…. Makes perfect sense."

It didn't, but I wasn't going to argue.

CHAPTER 9

SPAFFORD TEXAS –
BRAD

Y ou sure you're ok with this?" Stu asked.

"I talked to Maria and Marcy, and they're ok with it. Joe was the one who kept everyone safe. Not that this was a haven of crime until last night."

"Ok man; me, Randolph and the kid are going to head back with the goats. We'll be back tomorrow to pick you up and take Bucky."

Watching from the window, the men tried to load the goats into the bed of the pickup truck. Spencer and Randolph each got head butted in the ass to land face first in the muck and manure in the wet part of Bucky's run. Stu grabbed him in a headlock and barely got Randy away from him before he had to hurt or kill the stupid animal.

"Since you pacified him, I nominate you to ride

THE WORLD ON FIRE

in the back with the goat," I said, snorting.

"Naw, I think he can ride back there alone. I don't think Randolph is going to have Spencer come back. This killing has him spooked."

"I think you're right, the kid has every right to be spooked. We don't know what they were looking for or where they were going… Oh hey, Maria," I said as the little girl came out of the bedroom and crawled up on the bar stool next to Stu.

"Momma fell asleep again," she said, her eyes heavy with exhaustion.

It had to be close to ten o'clock at night, probably past her bedtime. I was getting tired. I'd spent the afternoon at the house with Stu helping out off and on. Randolph had poked his head in but Spencer wouldn't come in. He'd told Stu that he didn't want to meet somebody he was probably going to have to bury. It was morbid.

"You hungry again?" I asked her.

"Uh huh," she said.

"Are you hungry hungry," Stu asked, "Or do you want a candy bar?"

"Candy bar?!" Maria and I chorused.

"Jinxed," she shouted, pointing.

Her quiet demeanor had cracked earlier and she was smiling and joking with us now. If we were going to do anything horrible, she probably figured we already would have done it, not feed her a double adult portion of Mountain House dehydrated beef stew. I got Marcy to eat some as well, but she'd almost thrown it up, so we opted for some bouillon cubes and hot water.

"Here you go," Stu said, snaking his hand out of his pocket and handing Maria a Payday bar.

"Where'd you get that?" I asked him, stunned.

Stu looked at me and shook his head. Right. Randolph was Joe's friend, and they'd gone through the house and barn looking for anything that might be of value or use to the town. He wasn't planning on taking it for himself, but the people of Spafford were already in a bad spot. Several townsfolk had stopped in and asked to use the hand pump for their own water and he had obliged. In all, their best guess was twenty to thirty people left in town.

"Vending Machine," he said after a moment, smiling.

"If you find another one Mister Stu... wait, I had you for dinner?" she broke up into giggles.

He looked at me questioningly.

"Stu ate stew also," I told her, which made her laugh even louder.

"Honey..." Marcy's voice drifted out of the darkness.

"Ooops," she said and opened the candy bar as she slid off the stool and went to check on her mom. Tired, but smiling.

"So, about your guns," Stu said.

"Yeah, leave me the SKS and an AK with about five magazines. I've got plenty of my own ammo but I'd like to have a backup gun in case my SKS has a hiccup again.

"Good thing we were thinking alike. Let me

THE WORLD ON FIRE

go get you those magazines, and then we're out of here."

I nodded and I followed him to the door. I heard the goats bleating from the back of the truck which now sported staked sides, with the goats we were going to trade tied off. They could move, just not very far, nor very much. With me staying, somebody didn't have to ride with them back to town. Stu brought back a double handful of magazines and gave them to me. He gave me a bro hug and then left without words.

Why was I staying to look after the Garcia family? That was the question. It had to be done, but why me?

"Mister Brad, my mom is awake. She wants to talk to you."

"Ok," I said.

I'd lost my night vision watching the truck leave, so I felt along the wall and found my bag in the chair on the other side of the shoe rack. I found my emergency candle and screwed off the top and lit it. The soft glow lit up the rooms as I walked my way towards the bedroom that Marcy was in.

"Maria, you should be going to bed," she told her daughter, who hugged her tight and headed to her bedroom.

"Are you feeling ok?" I asked her, putting the candle on the bed stand so we could see each other.

"I'm feeling all kinds of better," she said. "Ate something bad the other day and couldn't stop getting sick."

91

"It's hard," I told her, "especially in Texas."

"Thank you for your help. You really didn't have to stay…"

"Ma'am, you can't get out of bed," I told her.

"I probably can, but I haven't tried. Actually, would you make sure I can get to the bathroom without falling? I think I've bruised every bone in my body already and I have to…"

"Sure, yeah sure." I told her.

It was awkward, but she made it down the hallway without tumbling. I put the candle on the sink so she'd have light and waited in the kitchen till I heard the toilet flush. I'd refill the tank later, but that was my signal to give her a hand.

"For a second there, I thought the power had come back," Marcy said, "When the toilet flushed."

"Yeah, I filled the bowl and tank with the buckets. I've got backups for you." I told her, "But it's goat water, don't drink it."

"Thought it smelled a little funny," she said smiling at me.

"You need to get some more liquids in you and, if you can, I'd like you to try some stew again."

"Is this what you do to all your dates?"

"This isn't a date, I'm not… I mean…" I was flustered and she let out a dry chuckle of her own.

"I heard you talking to Stuart earlier. Just teasing you. I think I know why you're doing this."

"Why?" I asked her.

"God has you looking out for us," she said.

"I'm not sure I believe in that, in him. With everything that's happened..."

"It doesn't matter if you don't believe in him," she said, walking towards a bar stool instead of the bedroom, "he believes in you."

She sat down and folded her hands, resting her chin on them. It wasn't an act of seduction or being coy, she was simply almost ready to fall over. I still had the leftover stew in the pot, as I'd been planning on eating it later, but it had dried out a little bit. I relit the burner and put it on, adding some more water.

"I guess that's ok with me then," I told her, "and Stu was right. Before the EMP, before the war or whatever this is, I was all about me. I'm a professional hunter and it was always an ego thing with me. Had to be the best at what I did, had to do everything the way I wanted. Like I said, it was all about me. Sharing and caring, hell, even marriage material... that was never in my cards. I was going to be the eternal bachelor."

"Do you have any coffee?" she asked after a pause.

"I've got instant coffee," I told her.

"Then you're marriage material."

We laughed quietly, trying not to wake her daughter.

"So are you still feeling nauseated?"

"No," she said after a pause, "I think the food poisoning worked its way out, but I had already lost too much fluids. I couldn't think straight."

"If you think me having coffee makes me marriage material, I think that's a good example of you still not thinking straight," I said with a grin.

She fell silent, smiling. Even sharing words with a woman was calming somehow. I did not feel any sort of attraction or affection towards her, other than wanting to do the right thing by her and her daughter. I mean, I felt bad. If we'd come a day later, Marcy could have been too far gone. As it was, she'd drank seven bottles of water before she'd even felt like she had to use the bathroom. She would have been in bad trouble if we'd been any later.

The stew started steaming and I gave it a few good stirs and then handed her a spoon and a hot pad so she wouldn't burn herself. She ate while I found my tin coffee cup and a foil pack of Folgers. It wasn't my favorite coffee, but it worked in a pinch and it came in single serving pouches. Great for back packing, hunting, hiking and prepping. Now, it had basically got me a marriage proposal. Even if she was teasing me.

The mug started steaming about the same time she finished the stew, so I made the coffee black and handed it to her and put water back into the pot to heat up again.

"You can't be serious," she said, "I think I'll bust if I have anything more than that."

"It isn't for you," I told her grinning and showed her the single serving packet of Mountain House.

"You like that stuff," she said.

"I have an addiction," I corrected, "But there's this twelve step program I heard about, not the one

THE WORLD ON FIRE

with God... but something about The Church of
the Flying Spaghetti Monster..."

"Are you trying to make me laugh?" she asked.

"No," I lied.

"Good; you've got to work on your jokes."

"I'm no good at this," I told her, "Small talk."

"You're doing just fine. You uncomfortable with
long silences?"

"Not really," I admitted.

"Same boat," she said, and sipped the coffee.
Her eyes rolled with pleasure, "Not too hot. I have
to be careful, I haven't had coffee in months and
months."

"I don't know if that's good for your stomach,
now that I think about it," I told her.

"I'm already feeling human again," she shot
back, "I'll stop if it bugs me."

"As opposed to?"

"Not bugging me?"

"No, as opposed to feeling human?" I meant it
to be funny, but again humor failed me.

"No. I think... I remember when you came in.
I thought you had done something to my Maria or
were about to. You carried me in here and you literally saved our lives." She paused, waiting for me to
say something but I didn't. Couldn't.

"And then you fed us, made sure I was on my
feet. I wasn't feeling much when you came in," she
said, "other than being confused and scared. Now
I am... full, content, sleepy." She took another sip.

I didn't know where she was going with all of

that, but I appreciated it. In the end it sort of made sense.

"You can go to sleep," I told her, "I'm going to sleep in the chair by the door."

"Tell me about those men who came," Marcy whispered, looking back at the door.

"One was Mexican," I winced, I'd been trying not to use that word, but I went on before I could embarrass myself further, "and the others looked middle eastern. They had AK-47s."

"Did your friend go and check to see where they came from?"

"Not very far, just a couple miles until he couldn't follow through the desert with the truck anymore. They didn't leave much in the way of tracks. Probably crossed the area and then walked along the roads till they found a meal."

"Do you think we are in danger here?" she asked, taking another drink.

"No, I doubt it," I told her, halfway lying, "no more than anybody else with the way the times are."

"You said Mexican, you mean Hispanic or do you mean from Mexico?"

I winced again. Here we go, I thought, I know I'm going to make myself sound stupid. I owed it to her to answer.

"I believe he was from Mexico. It was the clothing he wore, the brand shoes he had on."

"Then he would be a coyote, an escort. I wonder why he was escorting three men in?"

I told her what I knew about the coming war.

THE WORLD ON FIRE

The news was grim, but she took it well.

"So when I am ready to travel, I'll head out and go further north, when I can walk."

"I think we can do better than walking." I told her, thinking of the car we found in the barn.

§ § §

The door splintering startled me awake. I reached for my SKS in my lap when a bright light shone on me and a blow sent me and the chair toppling to the right. I felt my flesh tearing as another blow landed close to the one that had knocked me over. It was something sharp. I couldn't see, but I felt the crushing weight as somebody pulled on my arms. My body wasn't responding and the flashing of lights throughout the house were the only thing I saw. I heard the screams… The gunshot and a child yelling for her mother.

§ § §

My muscles hurt, and I felt like I had to puke. I had no idea where I was, but I could feel the wind and every time the bed of the truck bounced… I opened my eyes wider. I'd been tossed in the back of the truck with Maria. She was hogtied, gagged and on her side the same way I was. Three men were sitting near the tailgate by my feet with their rifles held up at the ready.

"You go back to sleep, or I'll put you there," a

BOYD CRAVEN

man said in broken English, noticing me move.

"Are you ok?" I asked Maria, who was staring at me silently.

"I think so," she said.

I saw a tear run down her cheek.

"Your mother?" I asked her.

She shook her head, "A loud bang woke me up and some men grabbed me. Then they put us in this truck." She started to cry.

"No talking!" A man who'd been standing in the bed near the cab kicked me viciously and the world went dark again.

I fought the urge to puke all over his combat boots and won after a long silent stretch of minutes. Instead I turned to look around. Two more men stood by the cab of the pickup. The paint was an old faded blue. It looked like the Chevy we'd passed walking to the Garcia's house. I'd assumed it was out of gas if it was there. Unless whoever these guys were, were the ones staying at that house.

When they'd kicked in the door, I had assumed it wasn't to talk about Jesus or the new brand of Tupperware they were peddling; without even seeing their faces I thought it was more likely the kind of men who'd been killed at Joe's house. Now in the faint light of dawn, it looked like I was right. Every person who was riding in the back of the truck with us looked Middle Eastern.

"Don't look at me." The foot wound up for a kick again and I tried to tuck my chin to my stomach just in case.

THE WORLD ON FIRE

Apparently the fake out was enough. As it was, every pothole and bump felt just as bad as the kick, but I was conscious for those, and the ride seemed to take forever. When we finally stopped, a lot of words were exchanged as the men left the truck and other voices joined in. Now, living and growing up in Texas, I was bilingual. We all were down close to the border. It wasn't that we had to be, it was just how things were. None of what I was hearing was English or Spanish.

"Them," somebody said, and I felt someone undoing the bonds at my feet.

I hadn't realized how tight the ropes had been tied, because as soon as they were let loose the blood flow caused pins and needles so badly that when they dragged me to my feet, I almost fell. As it was, I was already a bit dizzy. I heard screams and looked to see them attempting to cut the bonds off Maria.

"Let me," I yelled.

They ignored me, so I tried to yell again until I got the butt of a rifle in the stomach. I fell to the ground, almost heaving. I held my bound hands up to my face, maybe to try to hold my gorge back in, when I felt the sticky mess on my cheek. I pulled my hand away and wasn't surprised to see the clotted and half dried blood. From when they knocked me out.

"I said, don't touch me!" Maria said, and she sat down on the ground by me, her hands still tied.

They may have undone our legs, but they had

99

earlier tied our arms and legs together. Now, they took the long ends of the rope and started pulling. I staggered to my feet and Maria popped up before she got hit and started following. She was crying and screaming the whole way.

"Shut up, we are going to talk to Khalid. He will ask you questions. No lies," one of the men said.

Maria started reciting The Lord's Prayer softly in Spanish under her breath. If I believed, I might have joined in.

CHAPTER 10

They walked through Brackettville in the dark, electing to go straight through than detour. Normally King wouldn't chance it, but there was nobody out there and they expect to run into any of the forces of the New Caliphate anywhere near here. Latest intelligence had them further north and west. So they were caught a little off guard when they were past town as the sun was rising. They were trying to find a shady spot when King noticed a dust cloud moving in their direction.

"What is it?" Michael asked.

"Truck coming," King told him.

"How can you see that far?" Michael asked.

"When you've seen one desert…"

"You've seen them all. Great, it's a dust cloud

caused by a truck kicking it up from the sides?" Michael asked.

"Yup. Dust's too high to be a small car. Besides, everyone down here has trucks."

Michael smiled at that and nodded. For the most part, that was true from what little they'd seen. They started moving off the road and towards a brushy area to hide when Michael had an idea.

"Is there any reason we can't hitch-hike?" he asked.

"Suppose not, but we're leaving a footprint if we do."

"Two men on foot leave an impression, don't ya think?"

King thought about it. It went against his training and everything else, but he focused on one thought. He was not behind enemy lines like he had been in hot spots all over the world. He was right here in America. Over there, even friendlies were considered unfriendly. Over here…

"Do it," King said nodding towards the road.

They started walking, readjusting their packs to give them access to their long guns. King held out a thumb when the truck pulled into sight.

"Think they are going to stop?" Michael asked, mirroring the gesture and walked backwards the same way King did.

"They will or they won't," he said.

The truck seemingly grew larger in size the closer it got to them until they could make out that it wasn't moving fast. If it had been, it'd slowed down

THE WORLD ON FIRE

a bit as the dust cloud seemed to be dissipating. The truck put a blinker on and, when it pulled to a stop, the driver leaned out of the window.

"You two fellas need a lift?" he asked, his accent so thick that King had to run the man's words through his head twice before answering.

"Yes sir, that'd be appreciated, if you're going south?"

"Yes, a few miles but it'll be a few closer to where ya want to go?"

"Sounds good," Michael answered. "I'm Michael, this is King."

"King huh, well I don't got room in the cab for you both. If one of ya wants to hop in the back and another up front…"

"We can ride in the back, it's hot out and the wind will feel nice," Michael said, knowing that there was no way King was going to fit in that truck with the other two. He'd take up half the vehicle as it was.

"Suit yourself. I'm Randolph, this here's Stuart. We're headed to Spafford. Probably can take you a few miles past that if you want."

"That's fine with me, a few miles is half a day's walk," King said putting his bag into the bed of the pickup and then took his M4 off his shoulder and put it in as well.

Stuart was eyeballing them as they were getting ready to get in and he turned to watch.

"Those aren't civilian models," he said to King, who'd positioned himself in the passenger side.

103

BOYD CRAVEN

"Neither is your AK, son," King said.

Stu's eyes widened and then he nodded in understanding. One soldier to another. Michael turned to see what he'd been looking at and saw the gun rack on the roof of the cab. Two AK-47s were in it, alongside a scoped rifle. He didn't recognize the rifle, but it looked like something his father would have used when hunting. Not a military issued weapon. He hurried to get seated and the truck took off.

§ § §

Who do you think they are?" Stuart asked once the truck had picked up speed again, counting on the sound of the passing wind to cover his hushed words.

"I don't know. You recognized their guns though. What do you think?" Randolph asked.

"Military gear. Plus, their packs and camelbacks. The kid has some Molle stuff that isn't in circulation anymore. I mean, other than the guns... maybe they're national guardsmen?"

Randolph thought about that, "I don't know. The big fella looked a little long in the tooth to be active duty still, even if he does look like a black Schwarzenegger. The kid looks maybe 19. Something... there's something."

"They probably think the same about us," Stuart said. "What time are the others coming?"

"I put the word out. I'm guessing we're going to

104

THE WORLD ON FIRE

be having about ten men show up later on. It depends on how they get out here, it's going to be a bitch to backtrack everything."

"I know, and I tried already," Stuart said, "If we can pry Brad away from that senorita we should let him go with it. He's the professional hunter.

Randolph was already nodding his head. They rode in silence, chewing on many thoughts and made it to the outskirts of Spafford faster than either had expected.

"Somethings wrong," Randolph said.

Streamers of smoke rose, not big billowing clouds of a new or active fire, but the remains of a large one. One that was almost dead.

"I don't like the look of this. Stop the truck," Stu said in a commanding tone that Randolph hadn't heard from him before.

He pulled over to the side, making sure not to brake too hard and make the strangers bang their heads on the glass.

"This town?" King said as the two got out.

"Something's wrong," Stuart said reaching in and unclipping the AK-47s and handing one to Randolph.

"I been smelling smoke. Is that something new?" King asked.

"Yeah, we dropped a friend off here yesterday," Stu told them.

"Want backup?" Michael asked.

Stu got a good look at the kid. He hadn't noticed earlier, but the kid was strapped with a match-

BOYD CRAVEN

ing pair of colts, he just had overlooked that when he saw the packs and the M4s. The kid was better armed than any of them.

"Where y'all from? I can't place your accent," Randolph asked instead.

"Alabama," King said, "No place nice."

"Where you headed with that kinda gear?" Stu asked.

"Son," King said, "If you don't want us going your way, we're heading south towards Mexico. I don't mind moving on, if we make you nervous."

Michael stood there softly watching the exchange, in a tense silence.

"So is that a no?" Michael asked, tugging the chest straps on his pack tight.

"I don't mind," Randolph said, "Stu's just a bit jittery. We've had some problems in these parts lately. I think having a couple more guns at our side might make this old man feel better."

"Ok," Stuart said after a moment and nodded.

"When'd you serve?" King asked Stu suddenly.

"Still in, got stranded when the balloon went up."

King nodded, "Stick tight kid, or head towards the base in about two weeks."

"What?" Stu asked, "Why would you…"

Then it struck him, the gear, the guns.

"You're—"

"Just somebody passing through, willing to lend a hand. Making no trouble for you guys." King said.

"Leave it," Randolph said, "There might be

THE WORLD ON FIRE

trouble and I don't want to keep it waiting."

"Brad," Stu muttered under his breath.

§ § §

"Somebody tried to light this place," King said, walking into the house they'd left Brad at.

"How can you tell?" Michael asked.

"You didn't go in that bedroom. Don't," King said when Michael went to look, "You don't need to see that. Whoever it was, did something terrible."

The big man's hands were clenched and his knuckles popped audibly. Michael hadn't seen King angry like this before. Actually, he wasn't sure if he ever saw King anything but a picture of control, almost emotionless, except when he saw Sandra.

"Scorch marks on the floor," Randolph said coming out of the room, a sickened expression on his face.

"Any sign of Brad or the girl?" Stuart asked.

"Girl?" King said, his head shooting around to look at the young soldier.

"A girl found us yesterday, her mom was sick. Brad came over here to help and ended up staying. Mom was in bad shape. Heat stroke and bad dehydration."

"And they did that to her..." King wiped his mouth.

"It was like Talladega?" Michael asked and, without looking at him, King nodded.

"Maybe they're over at Joe's," Randolph said.

107

"The goat farm you mentioned?" King asked.

"That's the one."

"Let's go," King said.

Randolph and Stu exchanged looks and shrugged. Whatever King was talking about had disgusted him as much as the rape and murder of Marcy. Just inside the bedroom they'd found the plaster to the right of the door blown away by a handgun round, but no handgun was in the room. Just the corpse. King had kept Michael out of the room. Somewhere in the chaos, they had decided to try to burn the place. Judging by the scorch marks, they poured something on the carpet in the bedroom and tried to light a fire. They had probably left before smoke had smothered the fire. All the doors and windows had been shut tightly.

King followed the two men at a distance and Michael made sure to keep a distance from King in case they came under fire, so he wouldn't be lined up like Randolph was doing with Stu. The goat farm was closer than either of them had thought. They expected to hear the goats and see them. Instead, they found cut fences and no sign of anything and anyone.

"Even took his car," Randolph said.

King started walking, gave Michael a look and he followed.

"Where are you going?" Randolph called.

"South," King said, "Same as before, except now I am going to be on the lookout. You coming?"

"Let's all go in the truck," Stu said.

108

THE WORLD ON FIRE

"We have to wait on the other guys," Randolph said.

"You wait if you want," King said, "But they've got a girl. Either come or not; I'm going."

"Come on Randolph," Stu said, "Let's get the truck."

"It's suicide," Randolph said, "We're playing soldier here, these guns, those guys Joe killed. They're terrorists."

King stopped and turned around.

"You've seen them?" He asked.

"Yesterday, we found bodies. My friend Joe was dead and one Mexican Coyote and some middle eastern men. All early to mid-20s.

"Where are they?" King asked, "The bodies?"

"We dumped them in the desert, a mile that way," Stu pointed.

"Figure out if you want to help us or not, old man," King said starting to walk again, "but we're going that way and if we can find a lift along the way…"

Randolph sputtered but Michael and King walked on. After a while Michael stopped and looked back. The men were still arguing.

"Think they're going to come?" Michael asked.

"Yup," he said and kept going.

"Then why don't we wait?" he asked.

"I want to look at the bodies myself."

In about ten minutes they both had worked up a sweat again and Michael was tired. This was roughly the time when they had planned to sleep, and every day, until they slipped over the border and into Mexico. Instead, they were heading off to look at dead bodies. The vultures gave a pretty good indication they were on the right track. In another five minutes they left the road and followed the birds that had been taking off and landing.

Michael fought down his gorge as he saw the corpse. There wasn't four or five, whatever the old man had said, just one dead Mexican coyote.

"There were supposed to be more," Michael said.

"There was. Look at the drag marks," King showed him where a heel had scuffed a line in the dry desert hard pack, "And they went that way," King pointed.

"I don't see a trail," Michael admitted after a minute.

"Truck or Jeep. Probably a truck or three," King said, "Hard to tell, except there's two tracks."

"I'll follow along." Michael said and shouldered his rifle.

Both were startled when they heard the distant booming and rifle fire. It wasn't loud, but the wind carried the faint but distinctive sounds to King's ears.

"Is that…"

"No," King said, "That's way too far away. Maybe we'll be there in a day or two but it's in the wrong direction. Something else is going on."

"Do you think… are they attacking?" Michael asked.

THE WORLD ON FIRE

"Sounds like it. The first big push of the New Caliphate. Let's go."

CHAPTER 11

"Bring me the Americans," Khalid instructed his lieutenant.

"Right away sir," he said, and departed.

While he waited, he puzzled over the scant intel the team had found and the potential repercussions of what had happened in Spafford. They had gone to determine if Rishaan had been ambushed and killed by a much larger force. Instead, they'd found the bodies of his scouting team, along with the Mexican Guide. They had searched a nearby farm for any signs of activity and had found the freshly turned earth and had dug down enough to find the body of Joe.

But was there a larger force at play? That was the question. The auxiliary airfield had been searched and appeared to be totally abandoned as if it hadn't been touched in months, if not years. It was just a spare landing strip for a just in case.

"The prisoners," the lieutenant said and nodded for the two to come in.

Brad and Maria had been sitting and waiting for this moment. They had both been allowed to go to the bathroom and were given water, then their ropes had been traded out for zip ties, binding their wrists and palms together effectively.

"Please, sit," Khalid said pointing to two small stools.

They sat, uneasily. The girl looked terrified and evidence of tears streaked the dust and dirt on her face. Brad had cleaned up the wound on his head the best he could in the short time, but it was still dirty and congealed blood covered the scalp wound.

"Thanks," Brad said with bloodless lips.

Maria said nothing, looking to her fellow prisoner.

"Are you from Spafford?" Khalid asked suddenly.

"She is, I'm not. Brackettville's where I'm from." Brad answered for both.

"Interesting. Are you a soldier or American policeman?"

"No, I'm a hunter," Brad said confused, "Just come into town to help out a friend and do some trading for some goats for our town."

"And you," he said looking at Maria, "Surely you're not a soldier or police officer, are you?"

His tone was pleasant, but she never met his

eyes. She was shaking when she answered.

"No sir, I'm in first grade. My momma is sick, I've got to go back and check on her. Please?"

"Not yet," Khalid said, "I just want to ask you some questions. Are you from Mexico?"

Brad looked up at Khalid when he asked that, but Khalid just waved a hand, silencing him.

"No sir, I was born in Texas. My great Grandpa was from Mexico, but he talked with a funny accent when he spoke in Spanish. Kind of how you speak with a funny accent in English."

"It does sound funny, doesn't it?" Khalid said.

"Not ha-ha funny, like that TV reporter guy, or the talk show guy with the horse."

Khalid looked at her, confused.

"She thinks you sound British," Brad supplied.

"Ah yes, I went to Cambridge for a time, before I had to move. Now little girl, what is your name?"

"I'm Maria, and that's Mister Brad. He was helping us because my mom got sick. Please mister, I have to get back to check on her. Mister Brad too."

Khalid looked at Brad, and he nodded back to his captor in acknowledgement.

"How is it a hunter comes to one of the smallest towns in Texas, armed as you were found?"

"Why were we taken?" Brad asks suddenly.

Khalid rubbed his chin, straightening his beard in his hand before saying, "I needed information. If you give it to me, I will hold you here at this camp and leave you behind when our Caliphate moves on."

THE WORLD ON FIRE

"There's no way I can trust that," Brad spat, "Look what you…" he looked to Maria and then looked to Khalid.

"I do not have all of the information as of yet. I need it one way or another. Unlike some of my brothers, I do not believe in the more… unpleasant ways of getting my information."

"Could have fooled me," Brad snapped back and Maria shrank into her chair, tears forming. "I have a pretty good idea what happened after I was knocked out. I'll tell you whatever you want to know if you give your word, pray to Allah or whatever, that if I tell you whatever it is you want, the girl is safe and can go free when you're done with us."

Khalid considered it for a moment, "Do you want to go home, Maria?"

The little girl nodded.

"I will say this," Khalid told them both, "My ways are not the ways of all of my followers and soldiers. I will guarantee her safety until we are done with this area. What the advisors and coyotes do is of no concern to me. Now, I have ten minutes until I must leave to coordinate something. If your information is not accurate and concise, I'll turn the girl over to my men and only when she is done, you shall be. Do we have an understanding?"

"You're a monster," Brad said quietly, "If you go back on this, I'll hunt you down and…"

"Please, you are in no position to threaten me. Most men in my position would have had you beaten half to death just as a warm up. I have done no harm and I've done my utmost to not... frighten Maria. I will only ask once more, do we have an agreement?"

"Yes," he hissed.

§ § §

Brad and Maria were led to a separate tent. The center pole was dug deep into the desert soil with the ropes on the outside pulling the edges tight. It was to the central pole that both were bound, back to back, sitting flat on the ground. One of the guard's mouths curved up into a half leer and Khalid's hand flashed out, hitting the man in the side of the neck, dropping him to the ground. Stunned.

"They are to remain unharmed. If you have a problem with this, I shall eviscerate you myself and leave your corpse for the wild pigs."

The man paled and picked himself back up and nodded, "Yes Khalid," he said, all ardor gone from his expression.

"Sir, communications say they are ready," another man said, running up and handing the Commander a portable handset.

"Squad 3-7 redeploy to Laughlin. Squad Commanders, fire at will," Khalid said and threw the handset back at the startled lieutenant.

Brad and Maria watched as Khalid, the Spear of Allah, left. The guards moved out of their field of vision and the flap of the tent closed, leaving them

THE WORLD ON FIRE

almost blind in the absence of light.

"Did they hurt my mom?" Maria asked.

"I don't know for sure," Brad said, "I was knocked out."

"I heard her screaming and crying for a while. She isn't sick anymore, is she?" Maria's chest was hitching and, back to back, Brad could feel it.

"I don't think so."

"Who's going to take care of me if she's gone?"

The question and the way the raw emotion came out of the young girl's voice hit Brad like a hammer. Suddenly he had a big speck of dust in his eye and he couldn't wipe the moisture away. He tried to talk, but a frog was in his throat or he was choked up. Coughing a couple of times, he told her either the biggest lie ever, or wishful thinking on his part.

"I'll take care of you when we get out of here," he told her, "we'll find out for sure about your mom, I promise."

They both sat there and listened as in a distance mortars and artillery started firing. The deep thunks were the loudest things they heard, and it was at a distance.

"Are we going to get out of here?" Maria asked once her sobs settled down.

"I hope so, I pray to God and I hope so."

"Do you know the serenity prayer, Mister Brad?"

Together, they recited it.

BOYD CRAVEN

God, give us grace to accept with serenity
The things that cannot be changed,
Courage to change the things
which should be changed,
and the Wisdom to distinguish
the one from the other.
Amen.

CHAPTER 12

J ohn, this is Sandra, do you copy? Over?"

"John here," he said, smiling at the sound of the familiar voice coming in over the scrambled channel.

"Last minute intel has them coming for Sauz Mexico to hit Laughlin Airforce Base, do you read? Over."

"Oh yeah. Trust me, these boys are going to regret crossing the Rio Grande. Fixing to engage. Stand by Homestead, over."

"Over and out," Sandra said, the radio crackling.

"Boys," John said looking around the group, noticing Caitlin, "and ladies, it's time. Everyone have their positions and placements picked out?"

They all nodded. Each of the members standing around the small card table in John's mini-camp was one of the operators who had helped break Americans out of three NATO-run FEMA camps. Those camps were the most corrupt and, with the disappearance of Lukashenko, the abuses were likely to not happen again, ever. The other camps were being run differently, even if staffed by the emerging national guard or NATO. The new model on rebuilding was coming out of Kentucky, led by Sandra's husband as a matter of fact…

"Get your teams in place. We do not have enough men," he said and then nodded to Caitlin who was rolling her eyes, "and women, to stop this. I've already alerted Laughlin, and they have some Apaches they moved yesterday as a 'just in case' measure."

"How'd you pull that one off, sugar?" Caitlin asked her accent thick in the Alabama man's ears.

"I'm still a wanted man," he told the group, "but if I'm giving intel, they're at least listening."

"You hope," Tex said with a grin.

"They didn't share their plans with me," John said, "but I think they're at a heightened state of alertness at least."

"Instead of what?" Caitlin, the former model, asked.

"Instead of head in ass syndrome," Tex answered, and then laughed when she flipped him off.

"Hold on," John said, putting a finger over his earwig to listen harder, "Ok here comes the push. We don't have the numbers to stop them, but I want

THE WORLD ON FIRE

to bloody them and make them pay for every inch."

"John," Tex asked, "Sandra was asking earlier if we'd heard from the advanced team. I haven't, but I was wondering if you had any last minute intel?"

"No, I haven't. Whoever they are must have balls the size of this state though."

"Wait, you don't know?" Tex asked him stunned.

"No, who is it?" John asked, knowing he was going to hate the answer, judging by the way the couple in front of him were suddenly interested in their combat boots.

"Michael and King," Caitlin said when Tex didn't answer.

John wanted to stomp, curse and throttle the boy, but he couldn't. He didn't want to lose it in front of his team, but he was close to it.

"How do you know?" he asked finally.

"I was relaying messages back to the Homestead earlier when you were on call to Laughlin. I had one earlier from them, much earlier, and passed it on to Sandra. She wanted to know if they had checked back in, but I hadn't heard anything."

"What the hell are they doing? What was King thinking?" John was furious.

"Well, about that… Apparently King and Sandra have some history."

"Really?" John said mildly, trying not to let the anger and sarcasm boil over.

"He was her war daddy."

That stopped John dead in his tracks.

"Are you sure?" A chill ran down his spine,

making his skin break out into goosebumps.

"She said war daddy," Caitlin confirmed.

John ran his hands through his hair. He needed a cut and a shave, but he hadn't had time for that. They'd been fighting small sorties and worrying Khalid's scouting teams off and on for weeks. They had been planning to stage an assault team near Spafford where the auxiliary airfield was, but it was just an abandoned stretch of asphalt now, with the real action fixing to push across the border in their way.

"You seem to respect this Sandra," Tex said, "and if Michael is with the guy who trained her... You got no worries."

"What if he becomes like us? What if he becomes like me?" John said quietly.

Michael had already had to kill, on more than one occasion. The kid had a natural talent with the pistols, but the really dangerous part of the kid was his fearlessness. He was a quick study and had mastered just about anything he'd set his mind to. That made John think of his own son, and felt a pang of guilt knowing he was in a safer country than either America or Mexico now. Still, Michael had almost been like a second son to him and he didn't want to see him hurt.

"What, a good soldier, leader and man?" Tex asked, an eyebrow raised.

"If they're out here, where's his mother?" John asked, diverting.

They'd all grown close, but only John had

THE WORLD ON FIRE

known the whole family.

"I think she's at the Homestead. Some lady with the same last name was sitting in for David, with Patty teaching her how to work the comm gear.

John sighed with relief.

"We have the traps and the escape routes all set?" ge asked suddenly, changing the subject as things got uncomfortable.

"Gone over them a dozen or more times." Tex said.

"Good, let's get ready, because here they come."

§ § §

Portable mortars had been brought in by trucks and ATVs, and every member of the New Caliphate who marched, carried rounds for them. Their first strike would have to disable the airfield and the helicopters that were parked there. Many of the mortars had been set up days in advance, and teams left hidden in the heat, for the bugs and spiders to chew on as they waited. They knew the time was close, and they were anticipating the orders at any moment. Their biggest worry was if any of the aircraft were loaded out, or any of the Apaches took off, the New Caliphate's main thrust into the country would be thwarted.

"Begin operations," Khalid's voice spoke from the radio.

The first targets had been the helicopters. When they had been moved a day ago, the teams had moved some and then redone their aiming and measurements. Three teams all started launching at the two Apaches sitting there.

An air raid siren went off, and men on base started running. Then the mortars and Artillery opened up from a distance. The men of the New Caliphate rose up out of their hiding places in the desert and started marching the last mile to their targets, knowing that many of them would have to take over the mortar teams jobs if one should fall. Each carried at least one or two rounds to be dropped off to selected teams.

Explosions, gunfire and screams filled the air. Men on both sides of the fence died, but the losses from the shelling was horrifying. Many of the men and equipment had been stashed a long while back. Raiding teams had come and gone across many border states of Mexico probing, but this stretch had seemed to Khalid, the easiest way of flooding into the country, so the plans were drawn. When the cargo ships full of Jihadists landed, they moved en mass to designated points. The cartels had handled the organizing from the beach front and, other than food and day to day supplies, the New Caliphate had been armed for war.

"Sir," a voice with an Afrikaans accent told Khalid, "I'm getting reports of landmines and IEDs. Another force is attacking us from the East."

"What? How large?" Khalid demanded.

"Small, maybe twenty or thirty individuals."

"Wipe them out if they become more of a nui-

THE WORLD ON FIRE

sance," he said. "Our priority is to dismantle and disable that airfield and any equipment that can be scrambled."

"Yes sir. They seemed prepared for our guys on landing, but initial reports are showing that the artillery barrage has worked well. All helicopters are disabled and the airfield is being shelled to make it impossible to land a plane of any sort."

"Good," Khalid said, putting the binoculars back up and surveying from a distance. "Very good."

CHAPTER 13

"How many do you see?" Michael asked, putting his pack down.

"Two," King said, meaning the tent where they'd seen the two prisoners being held.

They'd almost moved out when the pair had been dragged out of the tent, but there was a sudden burst of activity and many of the men in camp had started breaking things down, or loading stuff into pickup truck beds.

"I count two myself," Michael said, "and about eight or ten more walking, but I can't get a good count."

King lowered his pack as well. They'd been kneeling, the powdery sand sticking to their sweat-soaked clothing and skin.

"Take a few mags. Don't rattle," he said, looking

THE WORLD ON FIRE

the boy over.

"You think I've got too much?" Michael asked.

"Probably. You're young. Maybe you like the pain."

"No, no sir," Michael said with a grin, "I've been watching the tent flap. When the leader walked out, they were sitting and tied to the center pole.

"Saw that," King said. "We either take the two men out silently, or we take on the whole camp. You any good sneaking?"

"Just what you've taught me," Michael said feeling for his knife, a bowie.

"Good. I'll go first, you back me up. If hell breaks loose, stick to the plan."

"No problem."

King looked the kid over and nodded. He'd shouldered his M4, but his colts were within easy reach. So was the big knife the kid had carried since day one after breaking out of the camp. He started moving slowly, using the natural brush to cover him, as he made his way closer to the camp. A lot of it had been taken down with the move, but the men who were left were packing up what remained, with exception of the command tent and the one where Brad and the girl, Maria, were being held. Everyone else was busy, so they weren't paying attention.

Neither was one of the guards. He'd pulled a stool up and rested against a support rope. His head kept nodding as he woke up and fell back asleep in a pattern that many would liken to an infant fighting off bedtime. Still, the other guard was the more alert of the two. He kept shooting disgusted looks at his partner and would kick at his feet until the sleepy man pulled a pistol and aimed it at him.

"Ok, here I go," King said.

King pulled the stiletto out of his boot, and advanced slowly. The alert guard had turned his back and started walking towards the command tent when King fell into step behind him. The others were looking the other direction and, when King grabbed the man, one meaty hand crushing his throat and picking him up, no one noticed. It was when the neck snapped that the sleepy guard looked up. Almost seven feet of ugly was staring at him.

"I—"

Michael moved quickly, plunging the knife deep into his back between the third and fourth ribs, one hand over his mouth. He could have crushed the man's windpipe like King did, but he had thought it out. When the man quit twitching, Michael pulled his knife free and rubbed a handful of sand on the blade before wiping it with his own pant leg.

"Why not his?" he asked as Michael started arranging the body.

"He went to go dig a hole and kill a tree," Michael said pointing with the bowie, "this one fell asleep." He kicked the powdery loose dirt over the blood so it wasn't so sharp.

The moist red liquid was swallowed by the dry sand immediately, and he pushed more over it so it wasn't obvious.

THE WORLD ON FIRE

They dragged the body inside the tent and dropped it in front of the man.

CHAPTER 14

I could tell that Maria had fallen asleep. The leering guard hadn't been back, and her breathing had deepened. I could feel the rhythmic rising and falling through her back and her soft snores should have been the first thing that alerted me. Truth was, I had been straining to listen so hard, I was now hearing things. I was trying to pick up the explosions in the distance, the rattle of gunfire and imagine if it was Khalid and his men getting cut down, or was our side? The sounds of the men outside had been confusing as well. He couldn't understand much of it, but when one of the coyotes had spoken up about making sure to pack the Commander's tent last, he got it.

They were fixing to move on. Would the Commander honor his promise? That I didn't know, and

THE WORLD ON FIRE

I looked around to see if there was anything I could do, or something I could use to get out of these zip ties that wouldn't hurt the girl. Then something curious happened. The back of the tent fluttered and I heard a gurgle, softly, but it was there. Maria straightened up suddenly, having heard it too.

"What was that?" she asked me in a whisper.

"Shhh," I said, "Liste—"

A man the size of a tank strolled in with a dead Jihadist under one arm and tossed him on the floor next to me. His head was twisted at a funny angle but, other than that, he looked like he could have been sleeping. With his eyes wide open.

"Don't look," he whispered to the little girl, and then pulled out a 9" stiletto.

"What are you— "

A younger man had followed him in and clamped a hand over my mouth and held a finger to his lips. Maria struggled for a second and then the pressure holding my hands behind me was gone. The young man nodded and put a hand in my arm-pit and pulled me to my feet. I was better than I had been earlier; the effects of the blow to my head had almost gone.

"Shhhh, I'm King," the big man said and nodded to his companion, "and Michael."

"Thank you mister," Maria whispered as I felt somebody take my hand. I felt a little pressure on my wrists and then they were freed. "You rescuing us so I can go see my mom? She's been sick."

"We're here to get you out," Michael said quietly.

131

BOYD CRAVEN

"They're going to notice the dead guard," I said rubbing my wrists to get blood flowing in them again.

"Guards," King spat, "Window dressing," he said, using his thumb to point over his shoulder.

"How many are left out there?" I asked, wondering if this was a suicide mission, or only delaying the inevitable.

"Half a dozen or a dozen," King replied and then held his hands to his lips to shush us, stepping to the side of the flap.

The tent flap parted and two men entered, their AKs pointed ahead. Michael and I put our hands up immediately and half a heartbeat later, Maria did as well. The two were talking in Arabic and I didn't understand them, but so intent were they on the three of us, they missed the elephant in the room. King surged and, like in a football tackle, he used his mass and power to push one man into another, causing all three of them to go down.

The kid was faster than me, and he was already moving with a big knife flashing. One let out a short scream that was cut off quickly with a spray of blood and all I could do was pull Maria close to me so she wouldn't see what had just happened. Outside I could hear questioning shouts.

"We gotta move. You know how to drive a dirt bike?" King panted.

"Yeah," I replied.

"Move." King pointed.

I followed and, almost as if it was a Kung-Fu

THE WORLD ON FIRE

move, King pulled the M4 around his body and started firing off three round bursts. The kid's hands went into what looked like a quick draw - yeah, that's exactly what it was - and he started shooting. I had missed that entirely; he had twin pistols, though he was armed with a rifle as well. I scooped up Maria to use my body as a shield and started running, following.

They were headed to the only other structure still standing: the Commander's tent. Three quick shots from Michael and two men who'd been loading a small trailer hooked up to a Honda 4trax fourwheeler fell. Parked next to it was a dirt bike.

"Neither of us can drive the bike," Michael said panting, "and King's too big to ride in the trailer."

King literally grabbed and upended the trailer, dumping it, before hooking it to the ATV. Shouts rang out somewhere behind me and I kept shooting glances over my shoulder. I couldn't see anybody, but that didn't mean they weren't just ducking and waiting for their moment. I did, however, see four dead bodies to the left of where we had exited the tent. So we had from zero to six men left to deal with.

"I don't want you to leave me," Maria said as I put her in the trailer with Michael.

"I won't, I'll be on that," I pointed to the dirt bike, silently praying that it was gassed and would run. "I'll be right with you."

"Are these guys like GI Joes? Mister King looks like the guy from the movie..."

133

BOYD CRAVEN

"Gotta move," King said, firing up the ATV.

I straddled the bike and prayed. It fired the first kick and I was relieved to see the filler cap showed a mostly full tank. When King took off, I followed. I noticed that Maria was in the front of the trailer with Michael in the rear, a pistol in each hand. He was going to be playing rear gunner while I was a no gunner. Just a moving target.

The ground was uneven and I had to dodge clumps of sage brush, but when I chanced a look over my shoulder, I saw two groups of men waving and red flashes of gunfire. Somehow, we'd done it and, barring a lucky shot, we'd be safe. When King opened up the throttle more as the land smoothed out, I followed suit. We drove for a long while like that and, with any luck we'd be out of Mexico in no time.

A dust cloud was kicking up ahead of us. King swerved off the two track we'd been following and slowed to a stop behind the outcropping. I pulled next to him and killed the buzz saw sound of the dirt bike's 2-stroke motor and looked over.

"Friends of yours?" I asked him.

"Friends of yours. I hope."

I frowned at that, looking behind us. I hadn't seen other ATVs or dirt bikes, but that didn't mean they weren't coming. Warily, I turned forward as first one and then another pickup truck seemed to materialize out of the haze of heat that made the distant ground shimmer. When the third truck came into sight I relaxed.

THE WORLD ON FIRE

"It's Stu and Randolph," I told them.

"Your friend Mister Stu?" Maria asked.

"I think so," I said putting the bike on its kickstand and walking out towards the trail.

"Stay here kid," King said and pulled his M4 off his shoulder and took position so he could shoot over a low spot in the rocks.

Michael took another position at the far end.

"What are you doing?" I asked, not believing that they were drawing down on my family.

"They could have stolen a truck. How do you know it's them?" King said.

That stopped me dead in my tracks and I turned back to stare at him. He was correct, of course; we'd been taken in a stolen truck.

"Just don't shoot until we know for sure," I admonished them both.

"If it's Mister Stu, see if he has another candy bar for me," Maria called.

I looked back and she was smiling. Was I doing the right thing? I didn't know, but I stood out and alone, ten feet from the two track, silhouetting myself. Almost as if synchronized the trucks all stopped and, when the dust had finished passing us by, I wiped the grit out of my eyes and saw Randolph with one sunburned elbow poking out of the rolled down window.

"Excuse me folks, how do I get to Albuquerque?"

"You're no Bugs Bunny!" Maria squealed from somewhere behind me, and Stu leaned forward and gave me a grin.

The pickup trucks were loaded with men and rifles.

"God it's good to see you," I said walking forward.

Stu and Randolph opened their doors and I met them in first one and then two bro hugs. They clapped me on the back, sending puffs of dust and dirt flying from our crazy trip.

"Likewise," Randolph said, "who's your friends?"

I turned, embarrassed that I'd completely forgotten about them.

"King is the big guy," I said pointing and King tipped an imaginary hat, "That's Michael," I pointed as he was holstering his pistols, and of course you both know Maria from town."

"Her mom…" Stu began.

"Gone?" I asked.

They both nodded. Around us, the pickup trucks were unloading and King, Michael, Maria and I stood together inside of a growing semi-circle of men.

"Sounds like war's all broke out," a man in an old International Harvester pickup truck said, and stuck his hand out. "Was that you?"

"No sir," King said slowly, taking the hand, "the New Caliphate is probably taking out Laughlin right now."

That startled everyone and it showed.

"Ain't somebody gonna go stop them?" another man asked, his hat almost comical in size.

THE WORLD ON FIRE

I'd been there as they were packing up. The camp had literally gone from thousands to hundreds and then a double handful in the hours we were there.

"There is too many. We need the Army or the Marines."

"You were there? You saw it?" Stu asked me.

"We were both in the temporary camp where the Jihadists were camped. We could hear the artillery going off."

"I should go," Stu said to me, "Check in somewhere. They're going to need me."

"Hold," King said, pulling his radio out and turning a dial. He put an earwig in and spoke quietly and then listened and turned it off, taking the clear plastic plug out of his ear. He whispered to Michael who nodded to him.

"Can you folks follow us across the border to make sure we don't break down? We don't want to lose the ATV or the bike. We can use it later for operations and, Stu, is it?" Michael asked, Stu nodded. "We have somebody you can check in with down here in a week."

"Who are you guys, really?" Randolph asked.

"We're from the government, we're here to help you." King said deadpan, and then busted up laughing when everybody groaned.

Soon, they joined in as well.

"Candy bar!" Maria yelled, holding up a Payday triumphantly.

Stu ruffled her hair and shot me a grin. It wasn't

easy to smile or laugh, but I had to take what little joy I could right now.

"This place where people are checking in… Are they taking volunteers?" I asked.

"Can you shoot?" Michael asked.

I snorted and nodded.

"You're in."

"Just like that?" I asked.

"Son," King said putting a big, weighty hand on my shoulder, "There's not many of us left. It's convert or die, or just die. They don't give many choices."

I thought about the cultured way Khalid had spoken to us, the promise he had made. How we would be left behind and spared. Was he telling the truth?

"I'm in," I told him, making up my mind.

—THE END—

ABOUT THE AUTHOR

Boyd Craven III was born and raised in Michigan, an avid outdoorsman who's always loved to read and write from a young age. When he isn't working outside on the farm, or chasing a household of kids, he's sitting in his Lazy Boy, typing away.

You can find the rest of Boyd's books on Amazon:
http://www.amazon.com/-/e/B00BANIQLG

Made in the USA
Middletown, DE
13 April 2019